Bolan found her in the tub, and knew that she was dead

Her killer had wrapped the body in a giant towel. The warrior's mind screamed that he had come too late, and still he forced himself to peel away the blood-stained cloth.

There was a ringing in his ears, and Bolan felt the old familiar tightness in his throat. He swallowed hard and rubbed a forearm roughly across his eyes.

Blinking, the warrior carefully replaced the towel, as if afraid to hurt her. The woman's blood was on his fingers now. Her blood was on his soul.

From the pit of his stomach, Bolan felt it rising, uncontrollably, a primal growl. Snarling, he rose and began to move toward the window.

The Executioner was rolling out in frenzy mode. God help the one who had slaughtered Bridget Chambers.

MACK BOLAN

The Executioner

DON PENDLETON's EXECUTIONER

MACK BOLAN

Defenders and Believers

A GOLD EAGLE BOOK FROM

W⦿RLDWIDE

TORONTO • NEW YORK • LONDON • PARIS
AMSTERDAM • STOCKHOLM • HAMBURG
ATHENS • MILAN • TOKYO • SYDNEY

First edition May 1986

ISBN 0-373-61089-0

Special thanks and acknowledgment to
Mike Newton for his contributions to this work.

Printed in Canada

An infallible method of conciliating a tiger is to allow oneself to be devoured.
—Konrad Adenauer

I have no interest in conciliation, and I will not let myself, my loved ones, be devoured. Let the tiger hunt begin.
—Mack Bolan

THE
MACK BOLAN
LEGEND

Nothing less than a war could have fashioned the destiny of the man called Mack Bolan. Bolan earned the Executioner title in the jungle hellgrounds of Vietnam, for his skills as a crack sniper in pursuit of the enemy.

But this supreme soldier also wore another name—Sergeant Mercy. He was so tagged because of the compassion he showed to wounded comrades-in-arms and Vietnamese civilians.

Mack Bolan's second tour of duty ended prematurely when he was given emergency leave to return home and bury his family. Bolan made his peace at his parents' and sister's gravesite. Then he declared war on the evil force that had snatched his loved ones. The Mafia.

In a fiery one-man assault, he confronted the Mob head-on, carrying a cleansing flame to the urban menace. And when the battle smoke cleared, a solitary figure walked away alive.

He continued his lone-wolf struggle, and soon a hope of victory began to appear. But Mack Bolan had broken society's every rule. That same society started gunning for this elusive warrior—to no avail.

So Bolan was offered amnesty to work within the system against international terrorism. This time, as an official employee of Uncle Sam, Bolan wore yet another handle: Colonel John Phoenix. With government sanction now, and a command center at Stony Man Farm in Virginia's Blue Ridge Mountains, he and his new allies—Able Team and Phoenix Force—waged relentless war on a new adversary: the KGB and all it stood for.

Until the inevitable occurred. Bolan's one true love, the brilliant and beautiful April Rose, died at the hands of the Soviet terror machine.

Embittered and utterly saddened by this feral deed, Bolan broke the shackles of Establishment authority.

Now the big justice fighter is once more free to haunt the treacherous alleys of the shadow world.

1

The underground garage was cavernous, its sudden darkness stifling in contrast to the sunlit street outside. The tall man rolled down his window and slipped a plastic ID card into the barrier gate's security receptacle. As the blind machine identified him and the wooden crossbar rose, he smiled and retrieved the card. The cavern's mouth enveloped him and he passed into the bowels of Mother Earth.

Below street level, he cruised between the rows of cars and empty parking stalls. Halfway down the second row, he backed the rental into a stall devoid of recent oil stains and shut the engine down.

He listened to the ticking of the engine as it cooled, observing his surroundings with a hunter's eye. Anemic ceiling lights did little to dispel the shadows; he waited while his eyes adjusted to the darkness, making sure that he was alone. When he was satisfied, he locked the rental and pocketed the keys, proceeding to the elevator.

The city was a jungle, filled with predators. The tall man was alert to any sign of danger as he moved through the parking lot, his steps echoing in the stillness of the tomb. Above him, the denizens of daylight went about their lives and jostled one another on the streets, exchanging glances, monosyllabic remarks, preferring not to touch and thus become entangled with their fellow men. One hundred yards away, across Fifth Avenue, the shadows were already growing long in Central Park. The dawdlers and lovers there would soon be seeking shelter elsewhere . . . if there was a haven to be found.

Mack Bolan sought no sanctuary in the urban jungle. He was hunting now, and he could almost smell the presence of his prey.

The elevator contained other scents. Cologne and claustrophobia, a whiff of urine stubbornly resisting all the Pine Sol that had tried to drown it out. He punched a button for the fourteenth floor and the car began to rise.

It had scarcely started its ascent when it shuddered to a halt, the lighted *L* for Lobby winking at him like a silent reprimand. The doors hissed open and a blonde in fur and leather came aboard. Her green eyes registered surprise at the sight of Bolan. Then her instinctive caution mellowed into curiosity as she pressed the button for her floor.

Her eyes were on him as the car moved upward, and she seemed about to speak, but Bolan's silence stood between them like a wall. She could not read his eyes behind his mirrored shades. There was something in the hunter's stance, his presence, that deterred her from initiating contact. When the elevator stopped on Six, she bustled out and on along the corridor without a backward glance. The soldier watched as the sliding door closed on her retreating back.

Bolan knew that she had smelled the danger, recognized it on some deep, subconscious level. She had known that he was trouble, though she would not have been able to express her feelings verbally. She might not understand precisely how or what she felt in Bolan's presence, yet she knew that it was best to hold her tongue, to let him pass her by.

She smelled danger, sensed fear.

When the elevator reached Fourteen, Bolan stepped out into the empty corridor. Bolted to the wall, a pair of numbered plastic arrows provided all the guidance he would need.

He was not really on the fourteenth floor, of course. It was a fiction propagated by the architects and airline engineers, who carefully forgot about bad-news thirteen when laying out their blueprints and schematics on the drawing board. A harmless superstition, sure. . . .

Thirteen was just another number to the Executioner. He did not put his trust in luck, but in preparedness. With that in mind he took a moment to triple-check the sleek Beretta autoloader in its rig beneath his arm. He left his jacket open for easy access to the weapon as he moved along the corridor, already homing in on his prey.

The plush Fifth Avenue apartment house was silent, seemingly deserted for the afternoon. Any tenants in residence were safely tucked away behind their multiple locks, enjoying their expensive solitude. They might have been aghast, even outraged, at the ease with which the Executioner had penetrated their domain, but they were oblivious to him outside their doors.

He paused outside the door of 14E and glanced both ways along the corridor, producing a manila envelope and jabbing at the doorbell with his index finger, waiting while the chimes played out their muffled round inside.

Mack Bolan did not know the name of his target. But he knew the tenant very well indeed, and for exactly what he was.

Among his brothers of the blood, he was The Face, assassin extraordinary, with a talent for assuming new personas as another man might change his clothes. A hundred documented kills, with twice as many rumored on the street, had given him a reputation that commanded the respect of ranking mobsters coast to coast. If only half the stories had their roots in fact, he was a lethal operator working on retainer for the Mafia's *commissione*.

A moment passed and the soldier felt a pang of fleeting anxiety, a fear that he had come too late. His information might have been inaccurate to some degree, although he didn't think so. Still, he might have missed his quarry, and—

A shuttered peephole opened in the door, and behind it the voice was heavy with suspicion.

"Yeah? What is it?"

"Message from the company."

Bolan held the envelope aloft, allowing it to partially obscure his face. The features would mean nothing to his prey, but then again, there was no point in taking needless chances when the stakes were life and death.

The tiny trapdoor on the peephole closed, and Bolan heard his quarry throwing back the dead bolts on the other side. The door swung open just a crack, and Bolan nudged it wider with an outstretched hand, alert for any treachery.

His target had retreated half a dozen paces from the door to give himself some combat stretch. His narrow eyes devoured Bolan as the Executioner stepped through the doorway, closed and locked the door behind him.

"You don't look much like an errand boy."

"Hey, it's a living."

But The Face was right. The messenger dispatched by *la commissione* had been a scrawny five-feet-nothing in his stocking feet, his courage emanating from the Army .45 he wore beneath one arm. It hadn't been enough, and he was waiting downstairs now, inside the trunk of Bolan's rental car.

The Face was starting to relax. He moved in closer, dark eyes flickering from Bolan's face to the manila envelope and back again.

"So, whatcha got for me?"

"You'll have to check it for yourself."

He passed the envelope across and watched as The Face registered surprise. The envelope was lighter than he had expected, lighter than a hefty wad of traveler's checks had any right to be. It might have been completely empty, except for the peculiar weight at one end . . . rough, irregular beneath the paper as the hit man traced it with his thumb.

He ripped open the envelope, upended it—and stared bewildered at the squarish silver object resting in his palm. A pin or amulet of some kind, with what seemed to be a bull's-eye in the center, and . . .

The Executioner had one hand in his jacket now, his fingers wrapped around the butt of his Beretta, but The Face reacted with a savage speed that Bolan had not anticipated. Snarling like a cornered animal, the mafioso swiveled, hurled the marksman's medal straight at the warrior's face. Bolan flinched instinctively, and felt it whisper past his cheek.

He had the silent 93-R clear of leather, but it was still inside his jacket when The Face collided with him in a flying tackle that propelled him against the nearest wall. The breath was driven from his lungs, and then the gunner's talon fingers found his wrist, wrenching, twisting, forcing fingers to release the autoloader.

They grappled in deathly silence, scrabbling at eyes and throats and any other vantage points available, overturning furniture, dislodging paintings from the walls. No time for threats or curses now; the two combatants needed every breath and every ounce of strength to prosecute their lethal contest.

The Face broke free of Bolan's grasp, stepped back and aimed a short karate kick at Bolan's groin. Seeing it coming, the soldier pivoted to take it on his thigh. Numbing pain exploded along his leg from hip to knee. He tottered, toppled, fell and saw The Face bearing down on him, lips drawn back into a predatory snarl. His hands fumbled with the buckle on his belt, twisting, pulling, to reveal a curved three-inch dagger, double-edged and deadly.

He came at Bolan fast and low, lethal steel protruding from between his fingers like a claw. His fist was cocked and ready for the hook that would open Bolan's throat and leave him sucking bloody spittle through a second, ragged mouth below one ear.

Except that the soldier saw it coming and rolled and twisted, bringing both legs up against his chest, ignoring angry shock waves from his battered flank. He marked his target, held it with a slight correction for the hit man's loping stride and then kicked out with piston force.

Both heels impacted on the mafioso's kneecap and he felt it give, the leg all rubbery and useless now. The Face could not suppress a strangled scream, and then his own momentum brought him down, his outstretched dagger furrowing the deep shag carpet.

The Executioner was on his target before the mobster had a chance to catch his breath. A strong arm snaked around the hit man's windpipe, cutting off the vital flow of oxygen to the brain, while Bolan used his other hand to pin the lethal knife-hand flat against the floor. Beneath him, his assailant writhed and twisted, almost rising to his knees before the soldier's weight across his back and shoulders bore him down. Twice more he tried, and twice more almost made it clear, but Bolan had his head wedged back and twisted to one side, the vertebrae and muscles straining to remain intact.

A final twist with everything he had behind it, and he felt the bones, the cartilage give way. As Bolan struggled to his feet, The Face was staring back across one shoulder at him, eyes already glazing over, tongue protruding from between his lips.

The Executioner retrieved his pistol, double-checked the action and returned it to its rigging. Swiftly and efficiently, he then began to take the room apart, aware that only moments might remain before an anxious neighbor, concerned about the sounds of struggle next door, telephoned the police.

Bolan dismissed the possibility and concentrated on his task. Into the bedroom first, where luggage lay open on the bed. Forget about the suitcase; it would be checked through by baggage handlers in any case. The flight bag was a better prospect, and he emptied it, recognizing passport, airline tickets and other travel documents.

But Bolan's adversary would not be traveling anywhere for some time to come, until his neighbors marked the rancid smell and telephoned complaints to management. Until the super had a look inside the living room—the *dying* room—and called the morgue attendants to carry him away.

A man who spent his life avoiding any vestige of identity, The Face would not be missed by anyone at first. There were no friends to be unsettled by his sudden death, and as for his employers, well, they would not realize that he was dead, that he had been replaced, until it was too late. They would be looking for the messenger, of course, but that would take them nowhere, and the Executioner would have his work behind him by the time they started adding two and two.

There was too damn much at stake now for Bolan to sit back and let the game go on without him. He was committed to play, and everything he was or ever hoped to be was riding on the line.

He pocketed the dead man's travel papers, taking time before he left to empty out the chest of drawers and scatter clothing aimlessly about the room. Returning to the living room, he circled the prostrate form to retrieve his marksman's medal from beneath the couch.

Bolan finished scouring the room and he was satisfied. To all appearances the tenant had been murdered by intruders bent on robbery, and with Manhattan's crop of unsolved homicides the overworked police might be content to let it go at that. If not, they would have to pierce The Face's many veils of anonymity before they found a motive that would lead to any suspect in the case. And by the time they got that far—if anybody cared to try—Mack Bolan should be finished with his work.

Assuming that the death game he was joining didn't blow up in his face.

Assuming that his luck did not run out as quickly and as finally as that of his assailant had.

The fourteenth floor had been the worst of luck for one professional exterminator. Now another was prepared to take his place, prepared to begin a death game of his own. There were no rules and anyone could play, providing they could meet the final tab.

As for Mack Bolan, he was buying in. With everything he had.

2

The Irish stewardess served a winning smile along with Bolan's after-dinner coffee, then moved along the aisle. The soldier settled back into his soft reclining seat and faced the oval window streaked with condensation. Outside the Aer Lingus 747, darkness and clouds hid the vast Atlantic from view. He slid the plastic shutter down and killed the reading lamp above his head. Eyes closed, he simulated sleep.

Four hours of flying time remained before the jet was to touch down at Shannon airport, and another hour of driving time, at least, before Bolan would reach his final destination on the ground. Instead of chafing at the bit, he forced himself to relax and use the remaining time to sort out the bits and pieces of the puzzle that he had in hand.

It was coincidence, of course, that he had learned about the meeting in the first place. There were long odds against the opportunity for Bolan to attend in person, posing as the mafioso "wild card" he had dealt with in New York, but that, too, had happened. As for the odds of his surviving, getting any mileage from the round-trip tickets in his pocket, well, the Executioner had learned that it was never wise to challenge fate. When opportunity arose, you seized it by the throat and wrung it dry before it had a chance to slip away. And you never wasted time to wonder how or why the opportunity had come your way.

Too many soldiers never got beyond the how and why before their time ran out, and Bolan had been racing hard against the clock from the beginning of his endless private war. To falter was to die.

His mind turned to the task at hand, mentally shifting the pieces of the puzzle until they formed the semblance of a picture—fragmentary but still the best he had until he stepped into the middle of the killing ground itself.

His man inside had taken pains to stress that this would be no ordinary summit meeting of the Mob. There would be more at stake than stateside territories here, and delegates would not be limited to hard-core mafiosi.

Bolan frowned, the blue eyes open now and staring into darkness as he mulled over the implications. It was to be an international assembly, held on neutral ground beneath the watchful eye of a professional security detachment. Security so far had been so tight that Bolan's inside man could only guess as to the proposed agenda topics and the identity of delegates.

Nino Tattaglia was not his man, of course, but rather Hal Brognola's. Living on the razor's edge between the Mafia and Justice, taking up the slack when Leo Turrin surfaced as a federal witness and as quickly disappeared into the Phoenix program, Nino had already paid his way a hundred times. Originally snared by an indictment charging double murder, he had joined the effort grudgingly, but over time had shown a brighter side beneath the sleaze. He was going through changes, evolving into someone who could hold up his head when he walked and look his mirror image squarely in the eye.

Tattaglia's contact with the Executioner was something else again, completely separate from his federal undercover role...and every bit as perilous if it should be found out by either the Mafia or the FBI. Since the blowup in Virginia, the government did not want any part of Bolan, and Nino's tie-in with the Man from Blood might be enough to get his ticket canceled if it came to light. As for the Mafia's reaction, Tattaglia had been around long enough to know that experts on the payroll had a way of making hell a down-to-earth reality.

There was plenty to guarantee Tattaglia his share of sleepless nights.

His previous meetings with Bolan had coincided with a Bolan blitz of Ernie Marinello's New York empire some months back and again in Baltimore. So far, Nino's cover was intact, and the warrior was alert for any sign of hesitation when he raised Tattaglia on the line.

Tattaglia had a pipeline to the ranking hierarchy of the Mafia, but this time the information had been scarce, and the accumulated strain of living on the razor's edge had been audible in Nino's voice when Bolan last spoke to him on the phone.

"So how's it going, guy?"

"It's hanging in. And how about yourself?"

"I'm waiting for my ticket to a summit meeting."

It had been a rumor, nothing more, the kind of rumble that you pick up in the underground, distorted in the telling, possibly devoid of substance from the start. But Nino had been compelled to check it out . . . and he had scored.

"They've got it set for neutral ground," the mobster had said at last.

"How neutral can it get?"

"Try Ireland on for size. They've got a place reserved in County Galway."

"That's going overboard."

"It might be, if the families were sitting down alone."

He had wormed the story out of Nino until the picture had been enough to raise the small hairs on his neck and send a chill along his spine.

The families would not be sitting down alone this time. In fact, from what Tattaglia had gathered, the stateside mafiosi would be only one of several factions gathering in County Galway to discuss mutual interests. The underboss from Maryland was short on names, but he had learned that delegations were expected from Sicily, the south of France, perhaps Colombia, with its immense reserves of pure cocaine. There had been rumors, unsubstantiated up to flight time, of an Asian interest in the meeting—and whatever that might mean was anybody's guess.

A host of grim scenarios were jostling for attention in The Warrior's mind. He knew, for instance, that Sicilian mafiosi had been recently supplying mercenaries to their cousins in *la cosa nostra*. Leaks on both sides of the ocean had imperiled that connection, and the sit-down might be used to good effect for mending broken fences, setting up a new line of supply.

Narcotics would be high on the agenda, certainly, with the Colombians and other "snow" birds ready to negotiate from strength for higher prices, bigger slices of the pie. If Asians were involved, there would be China white for sale, and spokesmen from the south of France meant Corsicans, with their connections to the Turkish poppy fields.

What else?

There was no way of telling until he made his way inside.

The Face would be his ticket in, and if the guy had never done another worthwhile thing in all his rotten life, he had a chance to even up the score right now. Behind his mask of anonymity, the Executioner was coming to the sit-down as a welcome and invited guest.

The wild card's late inclusion as a delegate had arisen from the paranoia and dissension of the stateside mafiosi. Bolan had contributed in no small measure to distrust among the brothers of the blood, harassing them on every side. Federal prosecutions and recruitment of informers in the ranks had done the rest, until the Mafia was trembling on the verge of large-scale and continuous internecine war.

At the moment, the Eastern families stood together, more or less, their power base being in New York City with assorted outposts lining the Atlantic coast from Newark to

Miami. The Midwest was in turmoil, leaning toward the East but staunchly independent when it came to voting policy on the commission. The South and West were something else entirely, perched upon the brink of anarchy with every capo for himself, and it was there that Bolan found his handle on the Irish summit.

According to Tattaglia, delegates to County Galway had been chosen on the basis of respective strength on *la commissione*. New York's five families, with nearly half the current seats, were dominant. A pair of delegates from Kansas City and Chicago had been added for a semblance of democracy, but no one had been chosen to protect the interests of the South and West.

Until somebody had suggested calling up The Face.

Without a family to call his own, he owned allegiance to the brotherhood at large, but someone had decided that he would be the perfect stand-in for the Sunbelt capos overseas. His single vote would represent a geographic third of the United States, and even New York's finest would think twice before they spoke out openly against a killer of his legendary status in the underworld.

For Bolan, tracking down The Face had been a blend of luck and dogged perseverance. Another day, and Bolan would have missed his prey entirely in Manhattan, forced to fall back on contingent plans that would have left him on the outside of the conference.

But he hadn't missed The Face, and now that hurdle was behind him. His entry fee was paid in blood, but he was still a long way from the finish line. And getting there could cost him everything he had.

This time around the Executioner would not be satisfied with hit-and-git. He meant to bust the summit meeting from the inside out, and that required a different level of finesse. This time, the warrior meant to know his targets, one on one, before he took them out. He meant to get inside their minds and look out through their viper eyes to understand precisely what they had in mind, precisely where they hoped to go when they got up and left the conference room.

Once Bolan understood the enemy, he could defeat them anywhere. Until he understood them, shared their secret thoughts, he would be fighting a defensive war and flailing blindly at the body of the serpent, never able to destroy the scheming head.

This time around he could accomplish more than simply picking off the emissaries of the mob. As an invited delegate he would be free to move among them, rubbing shoulders with the capos and their *consiglieres,* sowing seeds of discord in the ranks, clandestinely escalating the hostility and paranoia that existed between the various factions.

Bolan shifted in his seat, deliberately reining in his own enthusiasm. He could not afford the luxury of overconfidence. It was a killer at the best of times, and from experience he knew that cocky soldiers seldom left the field alive.

A fighting man could overestimate himself—or underestimate his enemy—and it was all the same. The error was fatal, either way, and Bolan knew that he would need his wits about him every moment for the duration of his mission.

It was a miracle that he had come this far, and Bolan didn't even want to think about the odds against his survival through the next two days.

He knew that nothing said or done in County Galway would abbreviate his everlasting war. If Bolan lived beyond the next two days, there would be other enemies to face, other battlefields to freshen with his blood. It was a law of human nature that the predators would seek their prey among the weak, the innocent. And as long as there were predators alive and prowling through the human jungle, Bolan had a job to do.

So he was airborne now, and bound in the direction of an emerald island where the worst of predators were gathering to organize their rape of all mankind. He had a job to do, and he would do it to the best of his ability, so long as he survived.

Mack Bolan knew no other way of life. He could no more forsake his duty than he could have voluntarily stopped breathing.

The killing grounds were familiar territory to the Man from Blood. He recognized the landmarks there; indeed, he had erected many of them himself.

The Executioner relaxed, and this time he did not pretend to sleep. At peace with what was coming, he slipped into the darkness of his mind and found a place called Home.

For another hour or two, the killing grounds would have to wait.

3

Bolan signed the Avis rental contract and secured his deposit with the credit card that he had lifted from The Face's flight bag in Manhattan.

The charge card bore a name entirely different from the one on Bolan's passport, but it didn't seem to matter. Neither name was his, and harried as she was, the Avis agent was not intent on checking any documents. A line of loud Americans in louder shirts was backing up behind him now, the fat man closest to him muttering about the sluggish service, and the woman was glad to wave him on when she had finished packaging the rental contract, handing back the borrowed card.

So far it had been easier than Bolan had expected, easier than he had any right to hope. The passengers aboard Aer Lingus were required to sign a "terrorist control card" prior to touching down at Shannon, but the flimsy piece of cardboard, handed to a smiling clerk along with Bolan's bogus passport, would not have deterred a traveling terrorist in the least.

Bolan waited to retrieve his single suitcase, with the Beretta 93-R carefully concealed inside, then waited in line for a quarter hour to change his traveler's checks to Irish pounds. With cash in pocket and his weapon near to hand, he moved along beneath the omnipresent Failte—Welcome signs which are the tourists' first encounter with legendary Irish hospitality.

The rental car, a Saab, had been reserved for Bolan—for The Face, that is—and it was waiting for him in the Avis section of the lot, gassed up, with keys in the ignition. Bolan stowed his suitcase in the trunk and slid into the right-hand driver's seat, delaying his departure for a moment while he checked the complimentary map of Shannon and the larger, more elaborate one he had purchased at a newsstand in the terminal.

It would be rural driving for the most part, with a run through the city of Galway ninety kilometers or so along the way. From there, another forty-odd kilometers to Cashel Bay, his destination.

He took a moment to reacquaint himself with driving on the "wrong" side of the road. It came back quickly, and the Executioner was glad to put the Shannon airport terminal behind him. He felt exposed, confined, among the bustling tourists on their holidays, their luggage plastered with decals, and peevish children whining at their elbows. It was good to be alone again.

He had been half expecting a reception party for The Face, and now he was relieved that it had not materialized. The soldier needed time to think, prepare himself for what would lie ahead, and he was glad to be on the road.

And yet, suppose there *had* been someone waiting for The Face? A silent, unobtrusive lookout, say, assigned to mark his passage through the terminal, perhaps to tail him from Shannon to his destination, making certain that the wild card delegate arrived intact.

Knowing that it was possible, at least, the warrior checked his rearview mirror. He decided to circle through the airport parking lot once more to see if he was being tailed.

Satisfied that no one had been tailing him, the Executioner proceeded through Shannon, bearing north and following the signs for N18, which would transport him out of County Clare and on to County Galway for his rendezvous with death. He merged with hectic traffic on

Newcastle Road, keeping one eye on the road signs and the other open for incautious pedestrians. A virgin right-hand driver might have panicked in the circumstances, but the Executioner's experience abroad made him a capable driver.

When he was clear of Shannon, running easy through the outskirts to the north, he pulled in to a petrol station, parked the Saab in back and shut it down. He unlocked the trunk, pretended to be searching through his bag and fastened on the autoloading pistol with its bundled shoulder rigging, hidden underneath a change of shirts. Inside the rest room, Bolan locked the door and removed his jacket, relaxing as he prepared to get himself in harness for the life-and-death encounter that awaited.

The 93-R came complete with special silencer, accommodated by the custom holster hanging upside down beneath Mack Bolan's arm. The standard Jackass rig allowed for maximum mobility with instant access to his side arm, phasing out the costly lift-and-drag associated with the classic shoulder holsters.

Bolan settled the rig across his shoulders, tried out the draw and made sure that none of it was visible beneath his jacket when he moved. They would be frisking him, of course, when he arrived at his intended destination, but until then, there was no point in advertising.

The signs of Ireland's war were few and far between in County Clare—a Garda checkpoint here and there, the scorched facade of a Bank of Northern Ireland where the bottle bombs had warped and melted plastic lettering—but bearing arms about the countryside could still attract attention and unwanted heat. The war, like Bolan's own, was everywhere.

From Shannon, north on N18, the countryside becomes a verdant, gently rolling wonderland, surpassing any poster on any tourist bureau's walls. The myriad shades of green were dazzling to the eye, the rolling sweep of endless hillocks broken by erratic, tumbled-down stone walls erected in forgotten years to mark the boundaries of rural farms.

Sod houses, roofed with thatch, were dotted all across the landscape, as if they might have sprouted from the earth itself, extracting nourishment through roots that reached down deep, below the surface layers of peat.

But time had not stood still in County Clare, nor in her sister county to the north and west. The soddies now were interspersed with modern, ranch-style homes and long trailers standing on concrete blocks. At one point, Bolan passed a caravan of trucks and campers staked out on the roadside, bric-a-brac and scattered auto parts displayed around the campsite, stock in trade for modern gypsies.

Mack Bolan motored on through Ennis, Gort, the other tiny towns along the way, their names unrecognizable in Gaelic on the highway signs. He gave the Saab its head, unwinding through the gears, and in an hour he had crossed the border into County Galway, homing on the target zone.

Bolan felt like an intruder here, an interloper, carrying his curse of death, his stain of violence, through a pristine land. The soldier had to take a moment and remind himself that it had been his enemies, not he, who chose the killing ground. He was compelled to take them as they came, and in the end, there was no decent place to die by fire.

At Gort, he cut northwest to catch N6 and travel on to the city of Galway, driving parallel to the Atlantic coast. The traffic here was sparse, mostly farm machines and horse-drawn carts, and Bolan held the rental at a steady sixty-five along the narrow, rolling track. He would be losing time again in town, but he was still ahead of schedule and he saw no need to push it now.

He entered Galway from the west, and followed merging traffic on around through Eyre Square, the heart of town. With a population of thirty thousand, the ancient port clung to its romantic past. Forever proud of its medieval Spanish ties from an age when Spanish galleons sailed to seek a land beyond the seas, the city cherishes the mark of the *hidalgos* in its architecture, from the older back-street houses with their courtyards to the celebrated seaside Spanish Arch. Columbus passed this way, according to the local wags, and tarried long enough to say a prayer at the old Church of St. Nicholas before he sailed west.

But Bolan came from the land across the seas, and he was searching for the savages who sought their sanctuary on the emerald isle. There was no haven on earth where they could hide from the Executioner.

Bolan, too, was a pioneer of sorts, forever seeking out another battlefront, another time and place to meet the cannibals and rout them from their burrows. Unlike Columbus, though, he had no hope of discovering a bold new world. Experience had taught him that the killing grounds were everywhere, and that the enemy could be found almost anywhere.

Newcastle Road, running parallel to the River Corrib's winding course, led Bolan past the university, a hospital and the tiny towns of Oughterard, Maam Cross and Recess, strung out like scenic pit stops on the road to Cashel Bay. Bolan made himself relax and soak in the peaceful atmosphere.

He had to overcome his mounting tension before he reached his destination. He recognized the signs, could almost smell his adversaries now across the intervening miles. But he would wait and meet them in due time. Right now, he had enough to think about.

Like getting into the summit meet, for instance.

Like adapting to his role with such finesse that no one in the hostile gathering would find him out or even suspect him of duplicity until the time had come to fling his mask aside.

Like getting out, if it came down to that.

But first things first. Getting in was the top priority.

In Vietnam, Mack Bolan had observed the simple truth that people often "see" what they expect to find in any given situation, and his observation had provided him with yet another edge against the enemy. On raids behind the hostile lines, he had occasionally adopted peasant dress, and found that Communist patrols often overlooked his Western stature, passed him by without a second glance because he superficially conformed to their preconception of the local scene. And later, when the war came home for Bolan with a vengeance, he had seen that Western eyes were every bit as blind when it came down to spotting ringers in the ranks, detecting a determined Executioner in mafioso's clothing. If you dressed and moved and spoke with the authority of your position, you would slip by undetected nine times out of ten.

But on the tenth time . . .

He pushed the morbid train of thought away, aware that now the odds—however slim—were actually on his side. No one inside the summit meeting would have seen The Face before, or even spoken to him, and that left Bolan's field wide open for a center sweep. He was an unknown quantity—a wild card, and that provided him with greater freedom than he had a right to hope for in the circumstances. He could damn well play it his way.

Bolan knew he would be without another friendly face across the table to back his play if anything went sour somewhere down the line. And something *would* go sour, if Bolan had his way. It was the reason he had come so far and risked so much already: to make the dream go sour for his enemies.

If nothing else, he had to let them know that they were recognized, that someone cared enough to stand and risk it all to see them fail. If nothing else, he was ready to spend his life in taking out as many of them as he could before the roof fell in around him, and the Executioner could lay it down without apologies.

But he had not come all this way to die.

The Executioner had come to *live*, and largely, in the midst of all his assembled enemies. He was living large right now, and in his heart, he knew it was the only way to go.

4

The final six kilometers of road to Cashel Bay unwound like a roller coaster ride. The plush hotel selected for the summit meeting faced the coast, located on a small, unnumbered road south of N59, midway between Oughterard and Clifden. Before he had proceeded far along the rolling, twisting cattle track, Bolan knew that anyone who sought solitude in Connemara, County Galway, would be forced to pay his dues up front.

He had turned off N59 at Recess, ignoring highway signs that advertised the Connemara National Park. A small herd of sheep, all painted blue in spots, observed his passage with the fine indifference of longtime residents who see the tourists come and go until they all begin to look alike.

But they had never seen a tourist quite like Bolan. And those who met him at the end of his excursion on the roller coaster would long remember him.

He pushed the Saab to fifty-five, despite the dips and hairpin turns. He could already feel the enemy ahead of him, a grim, malignant presence that attracted him like a magnet.

They would be waiting for him, for The Face, that is, with anticipation equal to his own. He knew the Eastern families would already be worried by his very presence at the sit-down, by his unofficial role as spokesman for the South and West. New York would not appreciate him in the least, and it was not beyond the realm of possibility that they—or someone else—might try to take him out right there.

The Executioner was not ignoring any possibilities, and when the time came—*if* it came—he would be ready with a few surprises of his own.

He had a few surprises for them anyway, no matter how the Eastern team reacted to his presence. And if they weren't suspicious of him now, of one another, Bolan meant to give them ample cause during the two-day summit.

A short kilometer to go, according to his highway map, and now the soldier realized that he was running out of time. He was committed now, as he had not been since he left the airport terminal in Shannon.

He had been wrong about the matter of commitment. Bolan realized that now with crystal clarity. He had been committed to attend the summit from the moment that he killed The Face in New York City. Earlier, in fact—perhaps as soon as he had heard about it from Tattaglia.

No, even earlier.

The soldier had been driving toward the summit meeting from the moment that he brought his private, everlasting war to American soil, so many lives ago. When he had recognized the enemy, decided that he could not turn away and hide his head beneath the sand, his course had been set. And everything that followed after, from his bloody "second mile," through the disaster of the Phoenix program, on to Cashel Bay, was preordained.

The soldier had no choice but to proceed, to face the dragon in its lair and do his best to strike off its grinning head with a clean, decisive blow.

The highway met the coast, began to curve more gently, dips and valleys softening, allowing an appreciation of the beauty suddenly displayed before his eye. The countryside so far had been like something from a fairy tale, but here, where land met sea, the stunning vista almost choked off conscious thought.

A rocky coastline lay below him. Beyond, the bay was like a mirror touched with fire, reflecting sunlight from a myriad of swells and tiny breakers. It beckoned him outward toward the vast Atlantic. Bolan felt the call, responded to it on a primal level where he lived and finally pushed it back into the deep recesses of his mind.

He had a job to do, and there was precious little beauty, precious little sunlight in his task. He had already traveled far to find the vipers here, in emerald Eden, and he would not let a glimpse of seascape change his course.

He gunned the Saab, deliberately wrenched his eyes away from Cashel Bay and back in the direction of the road. Another hundred yards, perhaps, around this curve, where trees and hedges rose to block the inland landscape from his view.

He was slowing even before he saw the sentries waiting at the gate: two men, decked out in woolen sweaters, denim pants and hiking boots. They both wore stocking caps, with curly hair protruding, and Bolan recognized the ski masks, ready to be lowered into place at any sign of danger on the lonely road.

They would be packing iron beneath the bulky sweaters, and there would be other weapons in reserve concealed behind the hedges, still within their easy reach. It was a simple stakeout, innocent to all appearances but effective. He could have taken them if he desired, but one or both of them would get a shot off before they died, and that would be enough to bring reinforcements from the house. If this was the only entrance to the grounds, it would be difficult for anyone except a seasoned jungle fighter to surprise the underworld conventioneers.

Bolan braked the Saab and nosed it between the leafy pillars of the open gate. There was no barricade, per se, although a cattle guard across the entrance would make sufficient noise to warn a lookout spotted anywhere around the grounds. The gunners looked like cool professionals to Bolan, now that he examined them up close.

"And can I help you, sir?"

The brogue was thick, authentic, and it sent a little chill along the soldier's spine as he handed out his passport, with the simple printed invitation that should get him through the gate.

Assuming that they bought it, that The Face had not already been discovered and identified.

Assuming that they didn't try to take him here and now, aware of his colossal masquerade, and force him to defend himself by attempting to blow his fragile cover into smithereens.

The taller of the sentries scanned his passport, read the invitation twice and passed both to his partner. The guys were pros, which meant not taking any chances. If he got past them, there would be other, harder tests to pass inside.

The invitation disappeared inside a denim pocket and the passport was returned to Bolan with a smile.

"They've been expecting you inside," the taller sentry told him. "Glad that you could make it, sir."

"My pleasure," Bolan told him as he powered the Saab across the cattle guard, iron grating loud and harsh beneath his tires. With a sidelong glance, he picked out the Thompson submachine guns, one on either side, that served as hidden backup for the sentries.

The Thompsons cinched it for him, taken in connection with the sentry's brogue. And he was angry that something of the sort had not occurred to him before.

The planners of the summit meeting were intent upon invisibility. They had selected a hotel renowned for its distinguished Continental clientele, and they had put security in local hands, of course.

They had employed the IRA.

And it would be another faction for him to contend with when he brought the house down. The Irish gunners would be standing duty here as mercenaries, bought and paid for by the Mob, but the hired guns would be every bit as deadly here as in the north, where others of their kind were fighting daily for the hell of it.

With the IRA, things were different.

Their presence here changed the odds and multiplied the hostile guns the Executioner would have to reckon with before he made his move. It whittled down the chances of survival and reminded him, unnecessarily, that he was all alone among the cannibals.

And Bolan wondered just how hungry they would get within the next two days.

The hotel—Cashel House—had been a private manor years before. Its owner then had been a botanist who passed his time collecting plants from all around the globe, as far away as Tibet, arranging them in gardens that had gradually expanded to devour the estate. The great house was a perfect centerpiece, set back behind a manicured lawn with wrought-iron furniture out front, its many open windows facing west toward the trees and sea beyond.

The Executioner knew the place was closed for about four months of every year, November through early March, and that it boasted twenty-three distinctive suites for paying guests, restricted to adults. For recreation, Connemara offered ocean swimming, tennis, golf and legendary fishing that attracted steady trade from sportsmen from Germany and France. The management was family operated, friendly to a fault—and now in grave danger.

The warrior told himself the danger had existed here before he came, but in his heart he knew that that was only partly true. The summit meeting was a risky proposition, but from appearances, it had been organized efficiently. It would be Bolan's job to light a fire beneath the pot and see what surfaced when the human stew began to boil.

He would be risking lives, though, in the process, and he realized that he would have to take precautions to guarantee that no civilians came to grief because of him.

It was a challenge, and if he blew it, Bolan knew that he would carry guiltless victims on his soul for the remainder of his life.

The sunken parking lot of Cashel House was hidden behind a copse, and Bolan coasted down the gentle slope and parked the Saab between two other rental cars. Unlike the stateside sit-downs, where conspicuous consumption was a status symbol for the delegates, these cars were all of moderate or compact size, without a Cadillac or Lincoln in the lot. The mental picture of a limousine attempting to negotiate the narrow Irish roads had Bolan smiling as he locked the Saab, retrieved his suitcase from the trunk and started back to the hotel on foot.

The grounds smelled fresh and green, the scents of myriad different flowers mingling in a conglomerate aroma that was almost overpowering. There would be other sentries on the grounds, and Bolan started looking for them now as unobtrusively as possible. A flash of camouflage fatigues above and to his left, accompanied by a rustling of movement, and he marked the soldier who had moved in close enough to check him out firsthand. His hackles lifted momentarily, and Bolan half imagined that he felt the gun sights trained between his shoulder blades as he proceeded casually toward the lodge.

If they were wise to him already, would they let him get this far? It was impossible to say, and there was only one way he could learn the answer. Go on with what he had already started.

As if he had a choice.

The Cashel House proprietor was waiting for him as he neared the tall front doors, one hand outstretched, a smile stretched wide across his face. And there was something else—a whisper of concern, perhaps?—behind the sea-green eyes.

"Good afternoon and welcome, sir." The owner's grip was firm and dry, a hand at home with honest work. "Could I be helping you with any of your luggage, now?"

"I've got it, thanks."

"Tha's grand. I'm Ian Duffy, and I run the place here, with the missus. And you're Mr . . . ?"

"Black."

"Of course you are. And hasn't everyone been looking forward to your getting here."

The undertone made Bolan think that everyone except the owner had been waiting for him with happy anticipation, but it was hard to tell exactly what the man was thinking, what he made of waking up one morning with an army on his grounds.

"I'll see you to your room, then, sir."

"Appreciate it."

Bolan followed him inside the lodge. The tall doors closed behind him with a click of grim finality. He was in, but for how long? And would he find a way out?

The Executioner attempted to relax, but he was living on the moment, alert for any challenge, any hint of danger in his new surroundings. He had felt the enemy before, and he could smell them now, as if their very scent of death and decadence had seeped into the walls, the carpeting, to mark their turf and warn the competition off.

He let the death spoor of the enemy enfold him as he followed Duffy down the L-shaped corridor to his room. He was inside, and for the moment that was all that mattered.

And as for getting out again—if it was in the cards at all—well, it was too early now to think about an exit.

The Executioner could not afford to push too far, too fast, until he had a feeling for the place, his fellow delegates, their mood.

When he was ready, he would pull out all the stops and let them know what trouble was about. When it was time, he meant to let them see the cleansing fire, and feel its heat.

When it was time.

Soon.

5

Mack Bolan's room was billed as a "luxurious garden suite," and while the soldier had his doubts at first, they vanished as he crossed the threshold. Spacious sleeping quarters opened on a sunken sitting room beyond a curtained archway, and the floor-to-ceiling windows offered a sweeping view of gardens, curving driveway and the sloping parking area. The windows were not screened; they would provide Bolan with another means of exit—or a decent field of fire.

The soldier dropped his suitcase on the king-size bed and peeled a fiver from his roll for the proprietor, but Duffy waved the bill away.

"It's taken care of, sir, but thank you all the same. We're serving supper in an hour, but you're welcome at the bar now any time, if you've a mind. An' if there's anythin' at all I can be getting for you, just ring down."

He gestured toward the bedside telephone, and for an instant Bolan caught that flash behind his eyes again.

It's taken care of, sir.

And what precisely would that mean in terms of cash or other benefits? In terms of threats?

The Executioner had just arrived, but he could feel a tension in the atmosphere already, radiating from the owner, from the silent doors they had passed in the corridor. He wondered who was behind those doors, securely tucked away in suites like his and waiting for the moment when they would be thrown together, friendlies and potential enemies alike, to hammer out a deal.

Now Cashel House was under siege. The occupying army had arrived, and their troops were presently prowling through the gardens, hastily securing the long perimeter against intruders. He wondered if the place was more a fortress or a prison, and he realized it didn't make a bit of difference either way.

Whatever happened next, he had already breached their first line of defense.

He stood beside the picture windows for a moment, staring at the garden. A furtive movement among the trees attracted Bolan's eye. A sentry dressed in jungle camouflage was pacing off a narrow trail amidst the trees. He was visible for just an instant and then was gone, but it was long enough for Bolan to identify the man as a professional, his weapon as an M-16.

The IRA was still receiving aid from stateside, and many of the dollars marked for war relief were spent on arms before they ever left the United States. The M-16 was no surprise, and it was safe to bet the other sentries would not be relying on antiques for their weaponry. The Thompsons he had noticed by the gate were relics of another age, another war, but here was modern hardware with a vengeance.

And he was dealing with a crew that knew its job.

The years of fighting house to house against the British regulars had honed the northern soldiers to a razor's edge. They often struck at shadows now, refusing to distinguish enemies from stray civilians, but they knew their killing craft; it was in their blood.

The Executioner would have to deal with them before his job was done, and that was fine. He had no love for terrorists of any side, but still, the IRA was not his major target here. The Ulstermen might pose an obstacle along the way, but they were secondary targets.

Bolan had less than an hour to prepare himself before the delegates began convening in the lounge. The evening meal would be a time of feeling out the opposition, taking stock of strangers and renewing old acquaintances. The warrior wondered just how many solid friends there were beneath this roof, and how much it would take to put them at each other's throat. With any luck at all, he would be able to find out.

A shower first, to clear the cobwebs out and wash away the dust of Connemara's winding roads. The soldier shrugged off his jacket and freed the sleek Beretta autoloader from its shoulder rigging, stripping down to skin and carrying the pistol with him to the bathroom. There, he left it on top of the toilet tank, within reach while he was in the shower.

It was doubtful that anyone would move against him so early in the game, but stranger things had happened in Bolan's everlasting war. If someone had come to Connemara predisposed against The Face or expecting him to rock the boat, then Bolan's new identity could get him killed. He might already be someone's target, but then again, that was a feeling he had learned to live with long ago.

He turned on the shower and waited for the steam to rise waist high before he stepped inside. With face upturned against the stinging spray, he let himself relax, the hours and miles of travel slowly melting from him like a cast-off second skin. He might have slept that way, luxuriating in the warmth that seemed to cleanse him from the inside out, but he had work to do.

A twist, and now the spray was icy cold, the steam evaporating like a summer mist at sunrise, leaving rivulets of condensation on the shower's porcelain and glass. When he was wide awake and on the verge of trembling, Bolan turned off the shower and stepped outside, his footprints puddling on the linoleum.

He was alone. Of course. But there was no such thing as being overcautious in the hellgrounds, where your first mistake could be fatal. You were careful, or you died.

And sometimes, you died anyway.

Bolan understood the rules before he joined the game, and changing them was not within his power. But he would not have changed them anyhow. He was accustomed to dealing with the savages on terms they understood, to meeting them halfway, and it had worked so far.

His battle plan, with variations, was simplicity itself.

Identify the enemy.

Then *isolate* him from civilians, in the killing ground.

And, finally, *annihilate* him, while you had the opportunity.

This time the enemy had taken care of one phase voluntarily without his help. The delegates were isolated here at Cashel House by choice, and thus far unaware of the impostor in their ranks.

It would be Bolan's task to mark the various conventioneers, identify their group affiliations, ferret out the goals and aspirations that had brought them all here.

And when that was done, when he had picked their brains as best he could for any useful battlefield intelligence, he would annihilate them.

The soldier dressed for dinner, picking out a quietly expensive suit that would accommodate his side arm with a minimum of show-and-tell. He was expecting someone to detect the weapon soon, and banking on the wild-card reputation of The Face, his solitary status at the meeting, to explain it all away. If he was asked to give up the weapon, he would comply, and seek another way to arm himself before he made his move.

When he was dressed, Bolan gave the suite a final scan, alert to anything he might have forgotten in his haste. There was no way to guarantee against intruders here, but he had nothing to conceal beyond his motives, and a search would leave the prowlers guessing, empty-handed when they left.

He did not bother shaking down the room for bugs, or checking for a wiretap on the telephone. He had no one to call in Ireland, and he didn't spend a lot of time in conversation with himself.

When he was satisfied, Bolan left the suite and locked his door, more for appearances than for security. The empty corridor led past a staircase leading to the second floor, and past the silent doors of other rooms that would, he knew, be occupied by now. He pictured the other delegates inside, crouched down and peering through their keyholes as he passed. It made him smile, but he replaced the smile with a hit-man scowl before he reached the lounge.

And Bolan saw at once that he was wrong about those silent doors. The other delegates—or most of them, at any rate—were waiting in the lounge, lined up against the bar or broken into tiny cliques around the several coffee tables, settled back in padded easy chairs. He made a casual scan on entering, then drifted toward the bar, alert to eyes that followed him from every corner of the room.

A perky barmaid served him a pint of Tartan and treated Bolan to a beaming smile. If she was feeling any of the tension that had seemed to dog her boss she hid it well, and Bolan hoped for her sake that the lady knew them only as another group of businessmen on working holiday. Her presence here, together with the other members of the staff, reminded Bolan that his strike, when it began, would have to be a surgically selective one, avoiding harm to innocent civilians.

He sipped the cool, dark ale and turned to face the room at large, pretending casual interest as he scanned the faces once again. A rapid head count made it thirty-three, and two more entered as he finished counting, one of them with an attractive woman on his arm. That seemed a breach of protocol, and Bolan filed the face away for future reference as he tried to pigeonhole the others by their looks, attitudes and speech.

He recognized the New York delegation instantly. They sat together at a table on the far side of the lounge, hunched forward over drinks and speaking softly to each other as they scrutinized the crowd. Their leader, watching Bolan from across the room, raised his glass in a salute, the corners of his thin mouth twitching upward in the semblance of a smile. The long, familiar face was setting off alarms inside Bolan's skull.

Joe Scalish, sure, and that proved out the rumors that had circulated after Ernie Marinello's death. Bolan and Scalish had never met, but Bolan knew the mafioso's face and reputation well enough, and his ascension to the Marinello family throne was no surprise. With Vince Scarpato dead and buried in St. Louis, all his soldiers buried with him, it was only natural. As for Scalish's presence here, at Cashel House . . .

If Scalish thought the sit-down rated capos in attendance, he was banking on some major action, the kind Mack Bolan had been hoping for when he took off from Kennedy twelve hours earlier. And if the other families had sent their dons as well, it meant they were vulnerable, both here and stateside. If he played his cards right, Bolan knew that he could damn near have it all.

But he was rushing things again. He concentrated on the others, nodding back to Scalish with a cool indifference. He didn't recognize the other New York delegates, but there were five in all, a spokesman for each family. And it was this contingent that The Face had been employed to guard against, while speaking on behalf of his employers in the West.

The Kansas City and Chicago capos sat close by New York, their attitude and shrunken numbers letting everybody know that they were standing in Manhattan's shade. Chicago's don, one Vito Esquilante, didn't seem to like it in the least, and from the scowl on his companion's face

the feeling was distinctly mutual. There might be trouble
here, and Bolan made a mental note of that apparent dis-
content as he swept his gaze around the room.

The recent arrivals were settled on a sofa near the entrance to the lounge, and Bolan scrutinized them casually.
The man in charge was balding, sour of countenance; his
age was indeterminate, but there was something of a military air about him, in his thrusting jaw and erect posture.
His sidekick was a slender weasel of a man, but it was still
the woman who attracted Bolan's interest as he studied
them from his vantage point beside the bar.

She was attractive—stunning, really, when he thought
about it—with a model's poise and grace in every move she
made. Her flawless face was framed by auburn curls that
spilled around her shoulders. The simple velvet evening
gown was midnight-black and fit her like a second skin.

The soldier wondered at her presence here among the
cannibals, and sensed that she was more than window
dressing to the man who kept a firm, proprietary arm
around her shoulders. Either that, or he was big enough
and bad enough to make up the rules as he went along, and
in the middle of the toughest company from several con-
tinents.

The crowd was multinational. A preliminary scan had
picked out Chinese, Japanese and two distinctive cliques
of hard-eyed Hispanics in opposite corners of the room.
The delegation nearest Bolan, standing at the bar, spoke
French among themselves, and he had marked them as the
Corsicans Tattaglia had mentioned on the phone. Beyond
them, seated near the picture windows, the Sicilian team
sipped wine in silence, studying the crowd.

A little tremor raced down Bolan's spine as he picked
out the three Vietnamese and did a rapid double take.
Their presence here could open up a whole new can of
worms, and he was running through the gamut of alternatives when someone nudged his shoulder gently, broke
his train of thought.

The barmaid let him have another of her sunshine smiles and handed him a menu, moving on along the bar to serve the Corsicans and the Sicilians in their turn. When she returned, he ordered salmon appetizers, soup, lemon sorbet and the veal cordon bleu. Still working on the pint, he passed on wine with dinner and she read the order back to him in her seductive brogue.

"Tha's grand," she said, beaming, when he nodded. She bustled off to place his order with the chef while Bolan casually resumed his study of the enemy.

The presence of the Vietnamese took the summit in a direction that he didn't even want to contemplate. Not yet, before he had the facts in hand.

Perhaps five minutes had elapsed before the owner, Ian Duffy, made his entrance through the double doors that opened on the dining room.

"This way, please, gentlemen." He caught himself in time. "And ma'am, o' course. We're after serving supper now."

He led the way, the others following, with Bolan bringing up the rear. The soldier would not have been shocked just then to find himself included on the menu for the feast, trussed up for roasting with an apple wedged between his jaws.

The sumptuous aromas from the kitchen hit him now, reminding him of how long it had been since he'd last eaten. His appetite took over for the moment, but the soldier's mind was never far behind.

He would be having dinner now.

But there was still a clear and present danger that they would be serving death for dessert.

6

The seating in the dining room was prearranged. Bolan was directed by a smiling hostess toward a corner table, near the windows. It was shared by Vito Esquilante and his Kansas City sidekick who, during the shift from room to room, had been subtly separated from the New York delegates and shunted to the rear, removed from any contact with the spotlight.

Which was fine.

Bolan did not seek attention here, not yet. As for the others, well, if they were feeling slighted now, so much the better for his cause. It would be easier to drive a wedge between the delegates.

He sauntered toward the table, standing for a moment by his chair and studying the mafiosi seated there before him. Esquilante returned the stare but broke the contact first, turning his rat eyes to the man positioned on his left. The Kansas capo raised an eyebrow, rolled his shoulders in a lazy shrug.

"You sittin' down, or what?"

Bolan glanced back across his shoulder, toward the New York delegation, as he took his seat.

"Seems like we got the part the cat dragged in," he said to no one in particular.

The big man from Chicago regarded him with interest. Bolan half imagined he could hear cogwheels spinning behind the florid face.

"I know you, don't I?" Esquilante asked.

"Could be."

"Aw, sure. You're—"

"Black."

The soldier had cut him off before he could begin to speculate out loud.

"That don't sound kosher," Kansas City offered, grinning with a mouthful of discolored, crooked teeth.

"What's in a name?"

"Tha's right," the capo of Chicago seconded. He had been drinking heavily already, and while he wasn't drunk, his breath was strong enough to keep the Executioner at bay.

"You here for Frisco?" Kansas City asked.

Mack Bolan eyed him coldly.

"Frisco, Dallas. I've got friends all over."

"I'll bet."

The squat Chicago mobster cleared his throat and treated Bolan to another whiff of the distillery.

"I'm Esquilante. Vito. Outta Chi." He cocked a thumb in the direction of his shadow. "That's Ernie Barboza, from K.C."

"Pleezta meetcha."

Bolan nodded, did not offer either one of them his hand. It was a time for moving slowly, feeling out the ground and marking any snares before it was too late.

Up front, Joe Scalish had a crystal goblet in his hand, and he was tapping on it with the handle of a fork, the ringing sound a signal for attention from the delegates. It took a moment for the conversation to evaporate, and then the capo from Manhattan had the floor. He set the fork and goblet down beside his plate and thrust both hands into his pockets, like a country politician speaking from the stump.

"I wanna welcome everybody here tonight, an' most especially the ones I haven't met in person yet. Before we get acquainted with the menu there, I thought we oughta get to know each other. Put the names together with the faces, so to speak."

A low, disdainful sound from Esquilante.

"Get this guy. He's a regular massacre of ceremonies."

The comment, and Barboza's soft, appreciative laughter, went unnoticed by the chair. Joe Scalish was enjoying his position in the spotlight, and it showed.

"Right off the top, I wanna introduce the man who put this thing together with a little help from his friends." A pause for laughter from the tables, followed by a sweeping gesture to the capo's left. "Alexei Gladnikov."

Bolan felt the short hairs rising on his neck as the late arrival from the lounge stood up beside his table, slick scalp shiny underneath the ceiling lights. He nodded to the room at large, looked properly embarrassed at the ragged scattering of applause, and then sat down again beside the stunning woman in the velvet gown.

A Russian.

And how the hell did that fit into any underworld scenario?

The answer was nagging at the Executioner already, skittering around the shadowed corners of his mind.

It would explain the presence of the Vietnamese, as well.

It would explain the IRA.

It would explain a lot of things.

The introductions were proceeding around the room, and Bolan marked the names as they were rattled off, committing them to memory for future reference, attempting to decide which delegates he might approach in relative security.

The Corsicans and the Sicilians had been seated close together, in a move that served to emphasize their connections through the trade in Turkish heroin. It would be difficult to drive a wedge in there, but not impossible.

A four-man Tokyo delegation represented the Yakuza, with interests in gambling and prostitution on both sides of the Pacific. There had been ethnic clashes in the States, around Las Vegas and elsewhere, and the tattooed men would be negotiating from the strength provided by their estimated hundred thousand members. Still, despite their strength they might be feeling paranoid among so many tried-and-true competitors, and Bolan thought he might be able to exacerbate that paranoia, given time.

The Chinese Triad team was something else again. They sat alone, away from their historic enemies, the Japanese, and Bolan knew their isolation in the room was more than just symbolic at the moment. The societies they represented had a lock on Asian heroin, the potent China white that was slowly displacing Turkish scag in the United States. An East-West drug war had been brewing now for several months; this sit-down might be aiming for a treaty that would open up supply lines and avoid expensive firefights down the road.

There would be little competition for the coke controlled by the Colombian contingent. They had been positioned near the table occupied by Scalish and the other capos from New York, as if to signify a bond uniting the Americas. Beneath the smooth exterior, however, there was tension and plenty of it. Bolan's job would be to find the necessary nerves and rub them raw.

The gaunt Vietnamese were hanging close to Gladnikov, the reason for their presence at the meeting still a question mark in Bolan's mind. If they were ready to begin discussing passage of narcotics through their ports, the Triads might be able to avoid the Bangkok markets, teeming now with undercover agents from a dozen different nations. It would guarantee protection until the smack set sail—and it would stifle any hope of marking shipments for reception stateside by the Drug Enforcement Agency.

But the Executioner suspected that there must be more than heroin behind the presence of the three Vietnamese. And his suspicion only deepened after Scalish introduced the pair of Hispanics seated on Gladnikov's right as delegates from Cuba.

The complexion of the summit meeting had begun to change before the warrior's very eyes. Bolan did not like the tinge of red that had been added to the color scheme. The Soviets, Vietnamese and Cubans would be running in a pack, he knew, and while the stateside syndicate had flirted with the Communists before in one guise or another, from Hawaii to the foggy streets of San Francisco, this would be the first time they had come together for negotiations on a formal basis. Bolan didn't like what was happening around him, but he forced himself to concentrate on Scalish, reserving all of the unanswered questions for later.

"We've got a chance to do some good here," Scalish told the delegates. "Like in the old days, right? Some of you may remember Charlie Lucky, when he sat down with the Jews, the Irish, everybody, an' they made a peace when everybody else was thinkin' small and killin' off the competition for some rot-gut booze."

He paused and looked around the room, allowing time for his simplistic parable to penetrate the densest skull.

"We've got a chance to go those guys one better here this weekend. If we play our cards right, we can make a peace *worldwide*, and that's the kinda peace that puts more money in our pockets all around."

A cautious ripple of applause, and Scalish raised his hands like a performer fending off his fans. Across from Bolan, Esquilante made a little retching sound and washed it down with wine.

"I know you all got things you wanna say, an' every one of you is gonna get his chance. That's why we're here. But right now, everybody's hungry, right?" A murmur of assent, and Scalish smiled expansively. "Okay. So let's find out if all this chow lives up to the advance publicity."

It did.

The salmon, paper thin and seasoned perfectly to Bolan's taste, was followed by delicious salad and the sweet sorbet. The veal was tender, succulent, surrounded on the plate by half a dozen vegetables prepared in different ways. Across the table, Esquilante and Barboza were already wading in, dispensing with their small talk now and concentrating on the food.

The Executioner ate ravenously, but his mind was on the information that he had gathered since arriving. For openers, he knew that this was more than just another gangland sit-down, since it had been broadened to include competitors from Europe and the East. The conference had a sinister potential that he hadn't grasped until the Communist delegates were introduced.

If the Vietnamese and Cubans were prepared to sign a working treaty with the syndicate, supplies of drugs and other contraband would be assured in perpetuity. And Bolan didn't even want to think about what the Soviets might be hoping to achieve from their participation in a worldwide crime cartel.

It fit, of course. The Soviets had been supplying arms and cash to terrorists around the world for years, without regard to ideology or goals. They armed the revolutionaries and the fascists with a fine impartiality, content to read their payment in the headlines that recorded rioting and random murder, the annihilation of the innocent.

Disorder was the game, and Moscow played it very well indeed. If terrorists in the United States were scattered few and far between, there must be other avenues of access to the nation's heart. Narcotics were a staple of the business, and a thriving syndicate—or syndicates—in competition for the trade would pay the Soviets a handsome dividend in propaganda headlines. Beyond the superficial threat, however, Bolan knew that pipelines built to carry drugs could carry other contraband as well.

Like arms, for instance.

And fugitives—or agents.

Assuming that Gladnikov was KGB, then Bolan was dealing with a different kind of threat entirely from the one that he had expected. And the soldier had to wonder just how much Joe Scalish and the other capos knew about the men whom they had welcomed to the dinner table.

It would matter little to the Mafia or to the other groups, of course, that they were dealing with the Communists. These men were opportunists, first and always, searching endlessly for ways to make a dollar or a yen on some illicit enterprise. And yet, they had a built-in sensitivity to being used and double-crossed, which should have had alarm bells jangling in their skulls when they sat down to reason with the KGB.

Joe Scalish and the rest would have some aces up their sleeves, damn right, and they would not be taking anything from Gladnikov on faith. There was a certain tension there, and it was something that the Executioner could work with, given time.

But the clock was running down, as always, and time was gliding by. Tomorrow, the next day, and the summit would be over. Any points he planned to score would have to be recorded in the next two days, or not at all.

The soldier cleaned his plate, but Esquilante and Barboza were professionals at eating, and they beat him easily, exchanging soporific pleasantries before they waddled off in tandem toward the lounge and giant mugs of Irish coffee waiting there. Bolan finished and thanked the waitress who took his plate, deciding he would give the bar a pass and take a turn around the gardens, in an effort to collect his thoughts.

Joe Scalish watched as he made his way across the dining room toward the exit, but the New York mafioso's face was unreadable. From all appearances, the guy was riding high on his association with the Russian, Gladnikov. That could work against him, too, if Bolan could find a way to turn the game around.

But he would need a handle first.

Dissension in the stateside ranks was good—the clash of East and West had worked for him before—but it would carry him only so far this time. There was a great deal more at stake than who controlled Las Vegas or Miami, and the Executioner would have to think in global terms if he intended to succeed.

Outside, a trace of sunlight lingered on despite the hour, fading slowly into dusk now, puddling dark shadows underneath the trees and shrubbery. Bolan chose a graveled trail, followed it along its winding course until he lost sight of the hotel. The undergrowth closed in around him, and he was alone.

It was a jungle out here, and in more ways than one.

The predators were out in force, and he would have to watch his step unless he wanted to become another item on the Cashel menu, served up for the dining pleasure of the cannibals. The first wrong move, the first false step, could be his last.

The soldier was at home with jungles. He had come to manhood in the Asian hellgrounds, fighting for his life against an enemy who rarely showed himself except in death. At home, when he took up his private war, he found a jungle of office buildings and expansive, tree-lined streets in place of twisting forest trails. But those jungles had been alike in the ways that mattered to a soldier on the move. Their snares, their predators, had been familiar to the Man from Blood, and he had moved among them as an equal, unafraid to face them on their own home ground.

The enemies from both of Bolan's wars were gathered here beneath the roof of Cashel House, and Bolan knew from grim experience that they were all the same. Complexions differed, dialects might change, but underneath the superficial masks, his enemies were savages, and they were all alike. Whatever ideology might separate or draw them close together, they were kindred, rotten souls beneath the skin.

And Bolan had a mission to eradicate them all.

He walked back briskly, listening for any sounds that would betray a tracker in the trees, and heard none. He was alone, unless the soldiers of the IRA were getting bet-

ter at their job. As Bolan cleared the trees and came in
sight of the hotel, he hesitated, blue eyes narrowed in the
rapidly descending dusk, his full attention focused on the
windows of his room.

The drapes were closed, but Bolan knew that he had left
them open when he went to dinner.

The lights were on, but he had turned them off before he
left the room.

He had been ready for a shakedown of the room, and
now he had a chance to turn the tables, score a few points
of his own. He circled around the north end of the wing,
avoiding entry through the lobby just in case a lookout was
stationed there prepared to phone a warning on ahead.
There was another door, which opened on the gardens at
the rear of the hotel, and it would put him back inside of
Cashel House a good deal closer to his suite. If there were
lookouts in the corridor, he would be able to surprise them
there, to get a look at them.

The corridor was empty, and he slipped inside without
a sound. The sleek Beretta filled his hand as Bolan stood
before the numbered doorway of his suite, one hand ex-
tended to try the knob.

It turned, the well-oiled tumblers opened silently, and
Bolan nudged the door wide open with his outstretched
fingertips. The prowler, intent on rifling the contents of the
suitcase on the bed, never heard the door swing open.
Bolan shot a sidelong glance in the direction of the bathroom, recognized that they were all alone and kicked the
door shut with his heel, allowing it to slam.

The prowler spun to face him, color rising in the cheeks,
one slender hand uplifted toward the cleavage of the mid-
night-velvet evening gown.

The lady's eyes were riveted by Bolan's own, the weapon
he held level from his face. He let her see the hunter's
smile, devoid of warmth.

"I'm very flattered," Bolan told her. "But I don't believe we've met."

7

"I can explain." Her voice was strained and breathless with the shock that he had given her.

"Why don't you try?"

"You won't need that," she told him, nodding in the direction of the weapon that he held.

The sleek Beretta's muzzle did not waver.

"Okay. So, where do we begin?"

"At the beginning," he suggested, moving closer so that she was forced to back away from him until she came up short against the bed.

"This isn't what it looks like, really."

"Ah."

"I'm not a thief."

"It never crossed my mind."

She tried a different tack. "I saw you in the dining room."

"You're wasting time."

"How much have I got left?"

"I'd say that all depends."

"On what?"

"On how much longer you keep playing dumb."

"You wouldn't shoot me here." But there was doubt behind the amber eyes, a subtle tremor in the voice. "It wouldn't be that easy to explain."

The Executioner allowed himself a narrow smile. "You're here without an invitation, and I caught you going through my things. I doubt that anyone in this crowd would ask for explanations."

It was sinking in, and she was going paler by the moment. And while he didn't plan on shooting anyone just yet, the soldier knew that she was close to cracking.

"All right," she said at last, "what do you want to know?"

"The obvious. Your name, your interest in my personal belongings, all that sort of thing."

A blush brought something of the color back into her cheeks. "The name's the easy part. I'm Bridget Chambers."

"An American."

It didn't come out sounding like a question, and she nodded an affirmative. "I get around. These days, I'm mostly in and out of France and Germany."

"Which side?"

The lady wrinkled up her brow, not understanding him. "Which side of what?"

"Of Germany. Your dinner date might not be welcome in the West."

Her face relaxed. "Oh, that. Alexei's welcome everywhere. He put this all together from the start, you know."

"That brings us back to you being here." He gestured with his weapon to include the room.

"I didn't plan to rob you, honestly."

"We've covered that. It's time for something new."

"Alexei will be missing me by now."

"He could be missing you forever."

"Oh, all right. He won't be looking for me, then. He knows I'm here. He sent me here."

It fit, and yet there was a hollow ring behind the lady's words, an undertone of something unconvincing.

"So what's his interest?" Bolan asked.

"His interest is the meeting, plain and simple. Anything and everything about his precious conference."

"I guess he has you searching every room in the hotel."

"Not quite. I think you've got him worried, just a little."

Bolan smiled. "He must be pretty insecure."

"I'd call it cautious, Mr. Black. He sees you as an unknown quantity, a—"

"Wild card," Bolan finished for her.

"That's right. He knows the others, from experience or by reputation. As for you, I take it that you're something of a mystery to all concerned."

"I like it that way," Bolan said. "It keeps them on their toes. It keeps me breathing, too."

"Alexei isn't very good at games. He likes to know exactly who his friends are, from the start."

"Is that from him?"

"From me. I don't want anybody hurt."

"I'm touched. Truth is, I'm mostly here to listen and report."

Her eyes were on the 93-R once again. "You came prepared."

"I used to be a Boy Scout."

"So, what happened?"

"I grew up."

"I see. And now?"

"I keep my hand in any way I can."

"Alexei thinks there may be trouble with your people from the States. A problem with the families."

"He might be right."

"And where do you stand, if it happens?"

"On my own two feet."

"An independent?"

"A survivor."

The look in Bridget's eyes told Bolan she had found a mental pigeonhole to place him in, all neatly indexed under "opportunists." That was fine with Bolan, but he needed more before he cut the lady loose.

"What's in this deal for Gladnikov?" he asked.

"Alexei is a merchant. He supplies . . . commodities."

"And now he's branching out?"

"It's only common sense. Suppliers need distributors, and competition drives the market down."

It fit. Too neatly.

"Okay, So what's your end?"

"I'm with Alexei." She pronounced the words as if they should have told him something.

"He doesn't strike me as a man who likes to share."

"You'd be surprised."

"So, everybody's happy, right?"

"I might ask you the same."

He lowered the Beretta, stowed it in the shoulder rig. Across from him, the lady visibly relaxed.

"I didn't come to rain on anyone's parade," he said. "Tell Gladnikov I'm interested in what he has to say."

"And your employers?"

Bolan shrugged. "They're businessmen. They'll listen when the money talks."

"Alexei is concerned about unrest between the families."

"That sounds like Scalish talking, now."

"They're friendly, granted, but Alexei doesn't follow anybody's lead."

"Does that include Department Five?"

"I beg your pardon?"

Something like a shutter dropped behind the lady's eyes, and Bolan knew that he had pushed too far.

"Forget it."

Bridget checked the jewel-encrusted watch she wore around one slender wrist and frowned. "I really should be getting back, unless you plan to rough me up a little first."

He smiled. "I'll pass."

Her smile was cautious, thoughtful.

"That's a pity," she replied.

And she was past him, out the door and gone before an answer came to mind. Her subtle fragrance lingered in the room, enticing and forbidding, all at once.

The soldier shook it off and double-checked the door to see that it was locked. One unexpected visitor was plenty.

The woman was something—one of several things—he hadn't bargained on. The Soviets, Vietnamese and Cubans put the meeting in a different light, and one that sent a little chill up Bolan's spine as he prepared for bed.

Alexei Gladnikov was KGB. Bolan had no doubt about it. If any proof was necessary, Gladnikov supplied it by his mere presence here, through his association with the other Combloc delegations at the conference. He would be acting under orders, and the knowledge of a Soviet involvement here, among the leading mobsters of the world, was chilling, sure.

An international cartel of criminals intent on moving drugs and other contraband was bad enough. But with a sinister, subversive element stirred into the equation, it possessed a devastating new potential, one the Executioner could not ignore.

He wondered just how much Bridget Chambers knew about her lover and associate. She hadn't tumbled to his mention of Department Five—the KGB's division responsible for sabotage, assassination, terrorism and the like—but there was something, hidden just behind the eyes....

He couldn't put his finger on it, but she did not strike him as a Soviet agent. It didn't fit. Still, he could not dismiss the possibility out of hand.

The Executioner had lived this long, against all odds, because he questioned everything, accepted nothing at face value. Experience had taught the Man from Blood to trust his gut, his instincts, but the ingrained caution of a savvy warrior held him back, prevented him from jumping to conclusions. If the woman wasn't KGB, she still belonged to Gladnikov and did his bidding in the face of peril to her life.

Or did she?

Something in her voice, her attitude, as she explained the rifling of Bolan's room, did not ring true. It was implausible that she would undertake the search alone, for private motives and unknown to Gladnikov, but then again...

The soldier shrugged it off for now. The riddle was a Chinese puzzle box, insoluble with the intelligence at hand. He would require more data before he cracked the mystery, and at the moment it was not his top priority.

But he would keep an eye out for the lady, yeah. And it would be a pleasure.

Bolan stripped for bed, his mind alive with strategies and angles of attack, a dozen separate scenarios competing for attention in the foreground. He had forged a link of sorts with Esquilante and Barboza over dinner, feeling out their anger and hostility, responding with enough enthusiasm to encourage the belief that they could count on him in time of need. It would remain for him to mingle with some of the other delegations, and sow the seeds of doubt, dissension, in inherently suspicious minds.

Joe Scalish was a target, certainly, but Bolan had alternatives to work with now. The Combloc delegates provided him with fuel, and Bolan knew that syndicated criminals—though hungry opportunists, totally devoid of principle—were basically reactionary anti-Communists at heart. Their pillaging activities were a bizarre perversion of free enterprise, and none of them had ever prospered under socialist regimes. Fidel Castro had closed the Mob's casinos in Havana, and other Red regimes had scourged their native narco-prostitution rings. If the Soviets were holding out an olive branch right now, there would be hefty strings attached.

Suspicion was a given constant when the gang lords got together, and with the Reds there as well, the mix would be intensely volatile. A single spark, applied strategically, could blow the KGB and all its friends sky-high.

A spark of Bolan.

But he would need some rest, some more intelligence, before he lit that fuse.

He wedged a chair beneath the doorknob, knowing it would not prevent intrusion but secure that it would give him warning, keep the enemy from catching him asleep and unprepared. He slipped the 93-R under his pillow, got in bed and pulled the crisp, clean sheets chin high. His right hand searched beneath the pillow, found the automatic there and closed around its grip.

The soldier was as ready as he would ever be. He needed sleep to clear his head, restore his strength and make him ready for another day among the cannibals.

Bolan considered every delegate to the convention, and his mind finally came back to Bridget Chambers.

She would take some time to crack, to understand. And time was now a luxury the Executioner could ill afford.

Instinctively, he shied away from striking at a woman, lumping her together with the rest, but grim experience reminded him that Evil had no gender. It came in every form, and many were pleasing to the eye.

Like Bridget Chambers, sure.

And if it came to that, if she turned out to be another of the cannibals, then he would handle her accordingly. With fire and steel.

The soldier cleared his mind and focused on sleep. He let the friendly darkness carry him away.

And in his dreams, he walked alone.

8

Bolan rose with the sun, reviving himself with a shower, dressing quickly, casually. The Beretta was concealed beneath a loose windbreaker, and he was carrying his valuables—the passport, cash—in case another visitor should drop by in his absence to peruse the room.

The Executioner was anxious to be out and moving before the others awoke and began to fill the dining room. He needed time alone in which to think about the coming day, the conference and, dammit, yes, about the woman.

She had been on his mind, but Bolan pushed her image back into the shadows and concentrated on the task at hand. There was a meeting set for ten o'clock with everyone attending, and throughout the afternoon there would be smaller get-togethers, ironing out specifics of a trade route here, a profit-sharing option there. Tomorrow's agenda was the same, with a concluding banquet in the evening—provided that the meet progressed that far.

It would be Bolan's task to sabotage the conference in the time available. It could be done, but if he was found out along the way...

Then what?

Should he expect to exit fighting through the ranks of hostile mobsters, through the IRA commandos stationed on the grounds? He didn't even have their numbers yet, and it was premature to think of breaking out alone, one gun against the scores of guns the enemy could raise against him.

Whatever he achieved today, tomorrow, Bolan knew that it would be achieved inside, within the enemy's ranks, and getting out was less important than hanging in.

The dining room was empty when he entered, but the smells emerging from the kitchen brought his appetite to growling life. His waitress from the night before emerged, all smiles, and showed him to the table he had shared with Esquilante and Barboza hours earlier.

"You're first today," she said.

"I like to beat the rush," he told her, answering the lady's smile.

"Tha's grand."

She handed him a menu, waited while he scanned and ordered, finally disappearing with a flourish through the kitchen doors.

Bolan thought about the coming hours. There would be pressure, for sure, and plenty of it as the day wore on. Right now, the Executioner was still involved in mapping out his strategy.

He knew about the tension in Chicago and the Windy City's satellites. It could be played to his advantage if he handled it correctly. As Michael Black, The Face, he spoke for families in the West, and there was room for more dissension there, if it should get around that California, Washington—perhaps Nevada, with its pot of gambling gold—were ready to secede. A blow like that could rock the conference, send it skittering off course, provoke a shooting war.

The waitress brought his food: fresh eggs, grilled tomatoes, bacon, spicy sausage, homemade bread and marmalade. The coffee that she poured for him was rich and dark. He thanked her and waded into the delicious meal when she was gone.

He was halfway finished when New York arrived, Joe Scalish leading, with the others straggling behind him like a string of pilot fish around a shark. The capo spied him instantly, eyes locked across the vacant room, and Bolan held that stare, resisting every urge to blink or look away, until the mafioso from Manhattan banged his shin against a chair. Distracted by the pain, he cursed and lowered his eyes. When they came up again, they had to deal with Bolan's coldest smile.

But it was kid stuff, right, this game of who-blinked-first. The Executioner was well aware that Scalish hated him—the man he was supposed to be—and that his presence here was like a needle in the hostile mafioso's flesh.

The thought did nothing to erase his smile.

He knew the others would be down to breakfast shortly, and he had no wish to see them yet, the woman least of all. He needed time to put the final touches on his plan, and Bolan finished quickly now, rising from his table as Esquilante, the capo from Chicago, bulled his way through swinging doors and found the dining room.

"You done already, hey?"

"I had an early night."

"Not me. Too damn much vino, that's for sure. Barboza's still asleep."

The soldier shot his eyes in Scalish's direction, taking in the New York crowd.

"Don't let him sleep too late. I got a feeling that we're gonna need his vote."

Chicago's little rat eyes bored into his own.

"You think they're setting somethin' up?"

"I think it's time Joe Scalish learned his place."

"You fuckin' ay. I like you, Black. We're gonna get along okay."

"I'm counting on it, Vito."

It would do for now and Bolan left him there, and emerged into crystal sunlight at the front of the hotel. In daylight, Cashel House was dazzling white, the flower gardens flaming with a riot of assorted colors. It was cool despite the sun, and Bolan was already glad that he had worn the jacket, rather than attempting to conceal his gun another way.

He walked toward the sunken parking lot and checked his car for signs of tampering, aware that he was being watched from the concealment of the trees. The IRA was on the job, protecting their selected guests from outside interference, and from one another if it came to that.

When he was satisfied that no one had been monkeying around with the rental overnight, the Executioner retraced his steps until he reached the sloping drive. Once there, he drifted right, away from the hotel and down toward the road.

Two sentries—different faces, now—stood at the bottom of the drive. The men were dressed for warmth, but there were bulky automatic pistols underneath their sweaters, and the omnipresent Thompsons would be somewhere close at hand.

"Good mornin', sir."

"So far."

"You'll not be leavin' us so soon?"

The warrior forced a smile. "A little turn around the beach. To settle breakfast."

"Ah."

They made no move to stop him, and the taller of them pointed out the railing fifty yards northward where a narrow walk was cut into the cliff, providing access to the beach and bay below.

"Be careful of your footing, there. It's treacherous this early, with the dew an' all."

He left them standing watch, and he could feel their eyes upon him, boring in between his shoulder blades like daggers as he made his way along the narrow road.

They would report him, certainly, and that was fine. The Face was known for unpredictability, for sneering at the rules. So far, he was in character.

Bolan reached the railing, spent a moment staring down at the idyllic stretch of beach below. It seemed to run for miles around the crescent rim of Cashel Bay, white sand and tumbled stone all scattered with the usual detritus of the sea. There was a boat far out where mist still clung to the horizon, but the Executioner would have the beach entirely to himself.

He started down the narrow steps, still mindful of the IRA commando's warning, well aware that an accident could take him out of action just as surely as an enemy assault. The steps were chiseled stone, dew-slick and treacherous beneath his feet, but Bolan reached the bottom of the cliff without a spill. After his precarious descent, the sand beneath his feet felt solid, reassuring.

He had an hour, maybe more, before the troops would finish breakfast topside and begin their business of the day. It would be open season then, with every mobster out for number one and anxious to secure himself a place within the new regime. A place as close as possible to the decision-making brains, of course.

It was a cutthroat kind of game, and one the Executioner had played before. The odds were longer now, the stakes increased, but he was not a novice to the game. He could compete with any of them—but with them all?

He ambled to the water's edge, the salt-sea air invigorating, crisp. The cliff behind him cast a shadow over Bolan, beach and breakers, blocking off the early-morning sun. It would be cool and shady here throughout the morning, a perfect place to hide himself away and let the hostile world slip past.

Except that he belonged up there among the savages, in the middle of that hostile world. It was a place that he had chosen for himself, and he could not forsake it now.

The breakers rolled relentlessly toward shore, each wave spent before it reached his feet. The beat went on like clockwork, never ending, and the Executioner could feel a strong affinity for that. His battle with the savages was never ending, too.

And there was no such thing as winning in endless war. The best you could ever do was hold your own, unless . . .

The metaphysics of it were beyond him, and the soldier let it slide. He was a fighting man, not a philosopher. His war was here and now, a thing of flesh and blood. The theoretical extrapolations of it could be left to someone else, some other time.

If there was no such thing as victory, there still must be the absence of defeat, and by surviving, by fighting on, he kept the long-shot odds at bay. The fact of his survival was a victory of sorts, and it would do, for now.

The bullet missed him by an inch, no more, and Bolan recognized its snap through empty air, reacting to the old familiar sound despite the absence of a gunshot echo in its wake. He pivoted, already breaking left and ducking low before the second round could find him. It would have split his skull, except that he was moving now, a target on the run.

The sniper had a silencer, that much was obvious, and from his vantage point atop the cliffs, Bolan should have been a perfect target. But the gunner had been overconfident or overanxious, and he had let the crucial first shot slip away. From here on, he would have to take whatever he could get—and Bolan wasn't giving anything away.

The sleek Beretta filled his hand as Bolan slithered behind the cover of a clutch of boulders midway up the beach. A rifle bullet creased the stone and ricocheted, its nasal whine evaporating over water in the distance. And another one burrowed beneath the sand a yard to Bolan's right.

He knew that it was hopeless if the gunner was beyond effective pistol range—and still he had to try. If he remained in place, the rifleman could starve him out, or pin him down while reinforcements made his meager stand untenable.

He had to move.

With the 93-R's fire-selector set on three-shot mode, the soldier edged to the right along the boulder's length and then came erect, propelled on piston legs, the autoloader braced in both hands, searching for a target, anything.

There was fleeting movement atop the chiseled staircase set into the cliff. A human figure was crouching, dark against the mottled green of reeds and other plants, sighting down the barrel of a weapon Bolan could not identify. He saw the puff of muzzle-smoke, squeezed off a burst in answer and was down behind his stony bulwark when the sniper's round made impact overhead.

The guy was out of range, and Bolan knew it. Worse, the sniper had to know it, too, if he knew anything at all.

The Executioner was trapped, a sitting duck. He could not remain immobile where he was. If he could reach the bottom of the cliff, he would escape the gunner's line of fire.

If he could cross the forty yards of open sand, devoid of cover, with the gunner sniping from his vantage point.

If he had strength and speed enough to go the distance.

He broke from cover, stroking off another useless burst toward the cliffs. The sand around his feet was sucking at him, slowing Bolan down and making him an easy target for the gunman overhead.

Except that no one took advantage of the easy shot. No whistling rounds descended from the heights to dog his footsteps, knock him sprawling like a dummy in the sand.

The runner faltered, broke his stride and stood with face uplifted, staring at the cliffs. He was a perfect target now, if anybody cared to fire. But there was no one on the staircase now, no figure visible along the rugged skyline.

Bolan was alone.

He altered course and approached the staircase at a cautious trot, the pistol in his hand. There still might be a trap in store for him, he knew, but he would have to put the beach behind him, scale the cliff, in order to confront his enemy. If they were running for it, they would have a lead that he could never hope to overcome. If they were laying for him now, prepared to open fire again when he was halfway up the narrow stairs, then he would die.

Either way, the Executioner could not afford to linger where he was, a standing target, isolated on the lonely beach.

Forgetting caution, Bolan took the steps at jogging speed, scanning the cliff above for the smallest sign of movement. A sea gull wheeled and mocked him with its silent grace, but no one challenged him before he reached the top.

The narrow, empty highway stretched away and disappeared. The steep embankment just across the road was overgrown with ferns and shrubs, their united green front unmarked by any sign of human passage. Downrange, the Irish provos were not visible, but Bolan knew they would be just inside the driveway's open gate, prepared to welcome any visitors.

He holstered the Beretta, smoothed his jacket to hide the weapon's outline and began the long walk back. It had occurred to Bolan that the sniper might have been an IRA commando, but the pieces did not seem to fit. The Ulstermen were hard professionals, employed to keep the meet secure, devoid—as far as Bolan knew—of any motive for assassinating "Michael Black" or any other delegate. In any case, they had the numbers and the guns to do a better job than he had witnessed moments earlier. If they had wished him dead, they could have tracked him down en masse, instead of sniping blindly, ineffectually, and then retreating out of sight.

The sniper's sudden disappearing act would indicate a predilection to avoid security patrols, and that left Bolan—literally—with a world of possibilities.

Joe Scalish came to mind at once, but it was early for the capo from New York to make his move. The foreign delegations shouldn't have a grudge against The Face, but then again, they might have been forewarned about dissension in the stateside families.

The Russian, Gladnikov, was another possibility, and that brought Bolan's thoughts around to Bridget Chambers once more. The lady could have set him up, reporting back to Gladnikov with God knows what interpretation of their conversation from the night before.

But would the Russian try to take him out so publicly, so soon?

A world of possibilities and perils faced the Executioner.

And he was walking back to them now, prepared to meet the worst his enemies could offer, and to give it back in kind.

The cannibals might eat him yet, but they would have to swallow him alive, and given half a chance, the soldier would devise a way to choke them in the process.

9

Joe Scalish cleared his throat and waited for the babble in the dining room to subside. Usually impatient, he had lately been struggling to cultivate the social graces, taking pride in how he almost never shouted anymore, in how he rarely used his fists to settle arguments where words would do as well. They said you couldn't teach an old dog new tricks, but this old dog was learning every day, and Scalish meant to go on learning everything he could.

The delegates were settled now, all watching him and waiting, like a small, respectful class with the professor at the podium. Except that this was Cutthroat University, your basic hard-knocks school, and all assembled here were graduates of an intensive training course. There was a good deal less respect among the members of his audience than Scalish would have liked, but that would come with time. And if it didn't, well, there might be ways to trim the class enrollment as they went along.

"I'm glad to see you all again," he said. "I guess the Irish coffee wasn't too strong, after all."

A pause for laughter, which was moderate at best, and Scalish forged ahead.

"Before we get to business, just a word about security." He nodded toward the rear, where Seamus Kelly stood, arms folded, smiling enigmatically. "We've got the best available, an' just in case you haven't noticed 'em, that doesn't mean they're not around."

A stirring in the audience, some furtive glances in the general direction of the IRA commando leader and his flanking bodyguards.

"You're free to come an' go at will, of course. This isn't prison, after all." No laughter now, and Scalish knew the cute was wearing thin. "But please use caution if you leave the grounds, an' show a little patience with the sentries when you check back in. They're here for you, an' they don't know your faces yet."

He paused and cleared his throat again. He would have liked to turn the clock back, start again, but it was too damned late. He was already in the middle of it now.

The faces turned toward him were impassive for the most part, and the mafioso wished that he could read the minds behind those pairs of eyes. The Asians were inscrutable, as always, and the Hispanics might have been asleep for all the animation they displayed. But they were with him, all the same.

No need for reading Esquilante's mind, of course. The asshole from Chicago made it plain he thought that he was getting screwed by experts, and Barboza, out of Kansas City, would be following Chicago's lead. There might be trouble from the two of them, but Scalish was prepared to meet the threat head-on, eliminate it ruthlessly, if they could only wait until the conference had achieved its goals.

The wild card was something else again. The Face was all alone so far, but he was speaking for a group of families who chafed against New York's restraining hand. He could upset the frigging boat if he decided things were going sour for his clients in the States, and Scalish might be forced to deal with him from strength. He hoped that it could wait, and yet . . .

"You all know why we're here," he said at last, commanding their attention with his voice. "Together, we're the upper crust of our profession all around the world. We got respect. We got the power, sure. But we could have a whole lot more."

Several delegates were leaning forward in their seats, listening to every word. And Joe Scalish knew that he had found the nerve connected with their wallets.

"Right now the competition's keeping us apart, an' keeping us from spreading out as big an' strong as we can be. We're steppin' on each other's toes day in, day out, an' that ain't good for business."

They waited as Scalish brought his message home. The Face, fat Vito, all of them were hanging on his every word.

"There isn't any reason why we can't cooperate, instead of buttin' heads and fightin' all the time," he said. "You think about the old days in the States, when whiskey was the hottest thing around, the families and different gangs were at each other tooth an' nail. The Jews and Irish, the Sicilians and the Polacks. It was years before they learned to live together an' bury the hatchet, but they finally got down to business an' forgot about the kid stuff, eh?"

He paused again to scan the faces of his audience before proceeding with the history lesson.

"It took some men with brains to end the wars an' put this thing of ours on solid ground. You got your Lucky Lucianos an' your Meyer Lanskys there. An' don't forget the others, like Bill Dwyer, Owney Madden. Hey, they had a regular United Nations by the time they sewed it up."

A ripple of appreciative laughter ran around the room and back again, encouraging the capo from New York. They were beginning to warm up, thank God.

"Today, this thing of ours is bigger than the old guys ever thought about, okay? But still, there's room to grow. We all got room to grow. There's no such thing as too much money, right?"

Scattered applause, beginning in the New York delegation, spreading weakly to the Corsicans, with Gladnikov lending a hand, smiling up at Scalish from the end of the banquet table they shared.

"All right, then, so we all want more. The point is, we can have it all if we stop fighting one another, stabbing one another in the back, an' just cooperate."

"Like how?"

The question came from Vito Esquilante, and the New York capo would have liked to throttle his Chicago counterpart right there and then. The bloated slug had spoiled his timing, ruined his delivery, but maybe at the same time he was giving Scalish just the opportunity he needed to make his point.

"I'm glad you asked that, Vito," Scalish lied, his plastic smile in place. "There's lotsa ways that it could work. The smack, for instance. It's our single biggest money-maker, right? Across the board? Okay. An' every time the feds bring down a major shipment, you've got panic on the streets until somebody finds an alternate supply. We have a problem with a foreign government, the whole damn operation goes on hold until somebody works things out."

They all were well acquainted with the problems, but they were waiting for some answers now, and Scalish let them wait a moment longer, watching him and hanging on his every word.

"Okay," he said at last, "so how's about we all cooperate and pool our sources, fix the prices to our mutual advantage, eh? The Turkish government comes down with an attack of virtue and the scag dries up awhile, no problem. We've got China white to see us through. The DEA cracks down in Singapore or Hong Kong, an' we've got our Corsican connection in the bag. They both get busted? Well, we've got some friends in South America who can supply the shit we need."

He had their interest now, and Scalish forged ahead before fat Vito or his sidekick had the chance to pose another question.

"Say that none of our suppliers gets picked up. What then? We've got the prices fixed, remember? An' we share the wealth, with territories laid out on the map for everyone to see an' recognize. There's no such thing as too much smack, you understand? Our present clientele can only handle so much, as it is, okay? The more we sell, the more new clients we create, not only in the States, but everywhere.''

His audience was silent for a moment, chewing over that one, watching him and glancing all around among themselves. They would be looking for a flaw, a blemish in his reasoning, but they would come up empty. Joe Scalish knew that it was foolproof, and he pushed ahead, excited now that they were hanging on his words like hungry peasants waiting for a crust of bread.

"Let's talk cocaine, all right? The feds are calling it the 'drug of choice' where I come from. These days in Hollywood, it takes a pound or two to bring a movie in on time, an' tha's just for the leading man, you understand?"

More laughter now, and they were with him—most of them, at any rate—beginning to reciprocate his own excitement, his involvement with the plan. *His* plan.

A smile from Gladnikov, and Scalish faltered momentarily, forgetting how to posture for a moment, realizing that it was a sham. And yet he had them now, he had the power. He would use it when he had the chance.

"We've got the biggest an' the best suppliers in the business here today." He gestured toward the slick Colombians, and they were smiling like sharks at feeding time. "They tell me they've got merchandise enough to go around, an' then some. We cooperate on transportation, distribution in our own respective countries, an' there isn't any reason why we can't do twice, three times the business that we're doing now."

The Colombians were fairly beaming now, enchanted with the thought of triple profits, and the New York mafioso sensed that he had made important friends already.

"Gambling has always been a major source of income for our families in the States. These days the rest of you are looking at it, too—your Monte Carlo, your Bahamas,

Port-au-Prince, Algiers. Las Vegas ain't the only show in town. If we cooperate, we've got the chance to organize a junket network all around the world, an' keep the suckers running through the system till they haven't got a dollar left to call their own. Together we could settle jurisdictional disputes so everybody stays in business an' the guns stay in the closet.''

Scalish sipped some water from a glass in front of him. He wished he had requested a podium for his address. The professional approach appealed to him, but it was working out the way it was, and in the capo's world, you didn't fix it if it worked.

"Somebody mention women?" Scalish asked rhetorically, and laughter answered him again. "The last time anybody tried a large-scale shipment internationally, it was the Tongs, like eighty some-odd years ago." A little nod in the direction of the Triad delegation, casually returned. "These days, you've got some half-assed A-rabs selling women on the auction block like swap-meet merchandise, an' then you've got your street pimps, hustling to make a dime.

"But we can change all that, if we cooperate. They tell me that we've got a hundred thousand people disappearing every year in the United States. A few of those, I know about myself." His grin produced reflexive laughter from around the room. "But half of 'em are women, see . . . or anyway, they're old enough to know the score. If we can tap that source—le's say we pull down ten percent—we've got five thousand working girls to trade each year. An' this ain't like the coke an' scag, you understand. It ain't some kinda one-shot deal. These bitches can be earning money for you over ten or fifteen years, you treat 'em right."

The room was silent now, the delegates involved with calculations in their heads. And every eye was on Joe Scalish, each reflecting dollar signs.

"Another area that some of us are interested in is guns," he said. "In case you haven't picked a paper up the last ten years or so, the world's not what you'd call a friendly place. With our connections in supply, the customers we have already for an outlet, we could move more hardware than the goddamned Pentagon. An' if we all cooperate, we can expand our markets all around the world. If someone wants to start a revolution, or they wanna put one down, they come to us. The main thing is, we can't keep usin' all that hardware on each other.''

Silence now, and Scalish noted that a number of the delegates were glaring daggers at their enemies around the room, each glance conveying blame and guilt for past hostilities. He had to take the edge off now, before the pot boiled over.

''I know it's hard to lay down these grudges,'' he told his audience. ''We got that problem in the States, damn right . . . and anybody says we don't, he's full of shit. We know about vendetta in the families, from Sicily right on to New York City. My old man got wasted in a street war twenty years ago, and there were times I thought that I was gonna spend my whole life playin' catch-up.''

Slowly, inexorably, he was winning their attention back. He had to hold them now. He couldn't let them slip away.

''So now I understand our friends from Tokyo are interested in some action stateside, but a coupla the families are standing in their way. An' there's some kinda beef between the Triads and the Yakuza that goes back, what, three hundred years? So, what the hell is that?

''We're talking futures here, and sometimes when you look ahead, you haveta kiss off yesterday. These grudges, this vendetta crap, it's bad for business, eh? I mean, what are we—businessmen, or half-assed punks still fighting for our turf?''

For just a moment Scalish thought he might have pushed too far, too fast, and then the ripple of applause was growing, spreading out across the room, surrounding him. The Japanese were nodding, and the Triad delegates were watching him intently, their impassive faces seeming to relax a little at the mention of a truce. He caught a glance from Gladnikov and knew the Soviet was satisfied, for now.

Scalish raised his hands to quiet the applause, and noted for the first time that the only one not clapping was The Face. His eyes were locked on Scalish, and the wild card wore a little smile, as if he might be looking through the New York capo, deep inside his guts, inside his mind, and tuning in on what he really felt right now.

The bastard was a menace and should be dealt with. Soon. Before he had a chance to touch base with the Western families and tell them what he thought about Joe Scalish and his plan.

A single holdout, even two or three, would not be fatal to the plan. They could be handled individually when the time was right. But if a territory half the size of the United States seceded, Scalish would be finished before he left the starting gate. With all his troops, he could not hope to tame the South and West together in a lifetime.

Better to sacrifice a single man and worry later on about the explanations he would need to pacify the absent dons. A scapegoat would be necessary, someone he could blame. Scalish thought at once of lard-assed Vito Esquilante. It would be a classic, eliminating two such vultures with a single stone.

The New York capo's smile was genuine as he addressed the delegates.

"I'm gonna let you go, now, an' I know you've got a lot of work to do. I'll be around to check on all the groups throughout the day, so if there's anythin' at all you need, don't hesitate to ask."

It was a casual dismissal, and the members of his audience were already huddling among themselves before Joe Scalish took his seat. In threes and fours they started filing out in search of other quarters, rooms where they could talk in private, garden paths where they could stroll and make their plans in daylight for a change.

The Face was halfway to the door when Vito Esquilante overtook him, tugging at his elbow, leaning close to whisper something in his ear. All right, Joe Scalish thought, that's what I need. The closer they appeared in public, the easier his work would be.

And they were almost making it too easy. Fat Vito was removing all the challenge from the game, but that was fine. At this point in his life, at this point in his plan, Joe Scalish didn't need another challenge. He for damn sure didn't need surprises here and now, when he was so close to finalizing all that he had worked for over eighteen months of sweating blood and kissing up to Gladnikov, as if the Russian was a god instead of just another sweaty foreigner with big ideas.

Joe Scalish had some big ideas himself. If they required some extra muscle, which Alexei Gladnikov was willing to supply, then they could deal. But when their dealings were completed, when the pipelines were in place, the Russian would no longer be essential to the plan. He was expendable.

Joe Scalish recognized no law beyond himself, no government except his own iron hand. If he could use the Communists to his advantage, fine. And when their usefulness to him was over, when he had the strength to stand alone, then bingo! Out like Lottie's eye.

He poured himself a glass of wine and sipped it, to keep from laughing. It was good to be on top of things. From where Joe Scalish sat, the view was fine and there was not a cloud in sight.

10

Don Giovanni Binaggio was a man of respect. He was accustomed—and entitled—to the deference of younger men within the Honored Society of the Mafia. From his youth he had earned that respect, that deference, in bloody contests that had always seen Binaggio emerge victorious.

He was a born survivor, and more. He was a winner.

It was not enough for Don Binaggio to coexist with his competitors. He had to dominate them, crush them if they offered him overt resistance. He would brook no insolence, no disrespect from men of lesser status in the brotherhood. As for outsiders, the civilians who milled about like mindless sheep, all fat and ripe for shearing, well . . .

Don Giovanni was a winner and a predator. The two went hand in hand, had always been synonymous with the capo's native Sicily. The strong were meant to prosper, and the weak to serve. It was a fact of life.

And Don Binaggio was strong.

He was the oldest and the most respected of the five Sicilian delegates at Cashel House, a figure to be reckoned with among the other men of power and respect from foreign lands. They visited his suite like minor nobles paying court, and he accepted their best wishes with the royal indifference of a king. They understood his place within the Mafia, his standing with the government at home. They would be courting him in earnest when it came down to discussing the supply routes for their precious powders out of Turkey, bound for laboratories in Marseilles.

If Don Binaggio should clench his fist one day, the pipeline of supply would be shut off, and all the dealers on the streets of cities half a world away, the armies of addicted slaves who bought their poison day by day would fall apart. He had the power in his manicured hand to strangle thousands if they did not show him the respect he deserved.

Of late, the Orientals had been challenging his strength, their Asian product turning up in cities and in veins that he had once supplied. It might have worried Don Binaggio if he was not a man of foresight and enduring patience. He had waited, measuring his enemies, aware that they could be allowed to push only so far.

And then, before he had been forced to act, his invitation to the summit meeting had arrived. The Orientals would be there, along with other men of power and respect from all around the world, and they would speak among themselves, resolve their differences for the common good. Binaggio had recognized the move for what it was—a masterstroke—and he was scarcely even jealous that the thought had come from someone else. He had accepted without the usual delay imposed to reaffirm his power when the capo dealt with his inferiors.

The invitation, in itself, had shown respect. The planners of the meeting recognized Binaggio for what he was, and left selection of the other delegates from Sicily to his discretion. Don Giovanni made his choices wisely, gathering the strongest of the other capos to him in a show of strength that would intimidate their rivals in the lower ranks. A solid front was necessary at the meeting, certainly, and they would have it, with Binaggio in charge.

He almost pitied their associates from the United States. This Joseph Scalish seemed to be a man of strength, but in America the brotherhood was scattered to the winds, with the local dons all running off in different directions. The warfare between the regional factions emphasized the lack of unity, the lack of leadership, and Don Binaggio had started wondering of late how anyone in the United States could call himself a capo with a sense of pride.

He might have cut them loose completely, shunning their company, except for the tremendous drug consumption of Americans. They used his heroin in quantities surpassing all the other nations of the world combined, and Don Binaggio would not cut off his nose to spite his face. He would soon be out of business if he should lose his massive market in the States.

Another reason why the summit meeting was important for Don Binaggio was that it allowed him to chart territories, draw borders the Orientals would not dare to cross. A man of patience, he was ready to be generous, but he was also ready to defend his livelihood at any cost.

He had been looking forward to a meeting with the Triad delegation and Scalish, the capo from Manhattan, when a tall, athletic-looking man approached his table on the sunlit patio. A gentle breeze deprived the sunlight of its sting, and Don Binaggio was feeling rested, generous, this morning. He decided to be patient with the stranger, just so long as the amenities were properly observed.

"Good morning, Don Binaggio."

"We know each other?"

A narrow smile, the eyes invisible behind reflecting shades.

"Not yet. I'm hoping that will change."

"You recognize my face?"

The stranger spread his hands.

"Who wouldn't? You're a famous man."

Respect.

"Siddown, siddown." He motioned toward the single empty chair across the table from his own. "I don't believe we've been introduced."

"I'm Michael Black."

Binaggio frowned, one eyebrow creeping up in the direction of his hairline.

"That's a name for an *amico*?"

His companions, Don Saietta on his left and Don Pariano on his right, picked up the joke and laughed appreciatively. Across the table, Giovanni's visitor relaxed the narrow smile.

"It's a name of convenience."

"I see."

The tall man was a soldier, then, and representing someone else. American, of course—the accent told Binaggio that, together with the clothes—but if he was not from New York...

"I need to speak with you in private, Don Binaggio."

A stiffening on either side, and Giovanni smiled, a big hand sliding out to comfort each of his attendant dons.

"These are my eyes and ears," he told the tall American. "We have no secrets here."

It was, of course, a lie, but it conveyed the proper feeling to his insecure companions, soothed their ruffled feathers for the moment.

"Certainly. No disrespect intended, sir."

"You show respect. That is good. What do you wish to speak with me about?"

"Our mutual interest, Don Binaggio. This thing of ours."

"I am listening."

"You know the way things are at home, my home."

Binaggio nodded, frowning slightly. "Go on."

"I wouldn't wanna see you get caught up in all of that."

"What has it to do with me?"

The soldier shrugged, a faraway expression on his face.

"It's possible somebody may be trying to bring you in, to use you in these troubles we've been having lately."

"Oh?" The capo's frown was deepening. "And why should they do that?"

"You're strong, you've got connections. Everybody knows. With you behind him, somebody could make a move, could maybe even make it stick."

"Does this someone have a name?"

The soldier smiled.

"I didn't come to tattle like a child in school. I'm speaking from the heart, and from the hearts of others who would hate to see you used this way."

Binaggio allowed himself a narrow grin.

"Could it be that you are using me a little, yourself?"

The soldier spread his hands.

"I'm just an emissary, Don Binaggio. I'm here to listen, and report on what I hear. This piece of free advice I give to you. I'm asking nothing in return."

"I keep your words in mind," the mafioso said. "And now, I got some business to attend to, eh? That's why I'm here."

"Of course. The best of luck in everything."

"I don't need luck." The lizard smile was spreading out across his wrinkled face. "I have respect."

The soldier took his offered hand and kissed the ring Binaggio wore. His eyes were visible for just an instant over the reflective shades. They were the cold, impassive eyes of an assassin.

"To your health," he said.

"And yours."

Binaggio watched the man's retreating back, one hand upraised to silence questions from Saietta and his sidekick, Pariano. There was much to think about, and little time in which to sort his thoughts. He did not need confusion added on to mystery at such a time.

The soldier had been warning him about Joe Scalish, that was clear. But why? What knowledge could this "Michael Black" possess about the machinations of the New York mafioso? By his own account he stood apart, a spokesman for a group of other dons outside New York.

And it was possible, Binaggio supposed, that some of them had planted him inside the meeting as a saboteur, to scuttle any plans Joe Scalish might devise.

The warning gave him pause. It was peculiar, this alert from total strangers, couched in cryptic terms.

Scalish would bear watching, yes. But Don Binaggio had worked that out ahead of time, aware that he could not afford to trust any of the stateside capos until the deal was finalized and put in action, tested by the fire.

For now, Binaggio would watch and wait. The test of fire was coming, and if Scalish failed, it would not be the man from Sicily who burned.

THE EXECUTIONER WAS SATISFIED with his achievement. He had planted doubts with Don Binaggio—or added on to those the mafioso had already—and the old man's face was showing tension when Bolan left. It was enough, for now, but he had a long way left to go before he brought the final curtain down. He was outnumbered here, outgunned, and he would have to light a fire beneath his enemies, turn them against each other if he meant to have a chance at all.

But first he needed contact with the outside world.

It had been nagging at him now since the shooting on the beach, a feeling that he might not be the only wild card there at Cashel House. A subtle undercurrent of uneasiness had stirred the small hairs on his neck, a combat instinct telling him that there was more in progress here than just a meeting of minds among some moguls of the underworld.

The KGB involvement was a part of it, of course. It added new dimensions to the threat and told the Executioner his savage opposition was evolving right before his eyes. He had a chance to stop that evolution, to set them back a year or more. But first, he had to satisfy the nagging in his mind that nothing else was going on.

And Bolan thought of Hal Brognola instantly. The fed might know if there was more behind the conference here than met the eye. If Bolan hoped to walk away, he would need some hard intelligence, and soon.

A meeting of this sort would not go undetected by the law enforcement agencies of different nations, certainly. Brognola must have known about the summit. Tattaglia would have tipped him to it instantly, before he answered Bolan's call. Around the globe there would be other Ninos, dialing other numbers from other pay phones, alerting other Hal Brognolas to the rumbles in the underground.

Did Brognola know that Bolan was a self-invited delegate?

Perhaps.

The fed would not have tried to head him off, in any case. No matter what was planned, no matter what was coming down, a dose of Bolan at the conference could only help confuse the enemy, prevent them from achieving their objectives.

Brognola had a job to do in Washington, and he was doing it, against the odds, without the necessary tools.

Like Bolan, sure.

They had been allies once. They still were friends. But each man had a war to fight, and they were not in lockstep anymore. The Stony Man debacle had demolished Bolan's government ties, and he was on his own.

Mack Bolan's friendship with Brognola had been honest from the start, and neither man had ever tried to con the other, even when their paths seemed diametrically opposed, as they did now. They shared a soul bond that was personal and indestructible.

Brognola would provide him with the information that he needed, once he knew that Bolan was inside. And he would use the Executioner, if possible, to further his designs.

Needing a telephone to call Brognola, Bolan knew without inquiring that the lines at Cashel House were not secure. They would be monitored around the clock—by Scalish, Gladnikov or someone else—if they had not been disconnected altogether for the weekend.

He would have to drive into town, and he remembered what the capo from New York had said. The delegates were free to come and go at will, as long as they cooperated with security.

The Executioner was feeling most cooperative now. He was the soul of acquiescence, perfectly content to play by all the rules.

Including some he meant to write himself.

Getting out, he knew, would not be difficult; getting back alive posed the problem. Someone had already tried to kill him once; his jungle logic told him that the shooter, having failed, would try again.

His outing provided the perfect opportunity. But it was also the perfect opportunity for Bolan to identify the hitter.

He was ruling no one out. Including hitters for the IRA, he had a minimum of fifty suspects on the grounds, and any one of them might seek to profit by his death.

He didn't know The Face—no living soul could make that claim—and he had no idea what ancient grudge the wild card might be carrying around.

The warrior veered away from sterile speculation, kept his feet on solid ground. He had a problem to resolve, and it would occupy his mind until a resolution was achieved.

He had to reach Brognola without delay.

He had to leave the grounds, touch base and return without arousing curiosity.

He had to make his run, and make it home alive.

And that, he knew, was going to be the challenge of them all.

11

Mack Bolan put the Saab in neutral, coasted down the final fifty feet of sloping drive and braked gently at the gate. The sentries were waiting, caution visible beneath superficial smiles.

"Will ye be leavin', sir?"

"I want to take a look around the countryside," he said. "I shouldn't be too long."

The sentries glanced at one another and back at Bolan, obviously unprepared to deal with anyone who tried to leave the conference ahead of time.

"Feel free to check with Mr. Scalish, if you like."

That did it, and the taller of them shook his head.

"Tha' won't be necessary, sir. Enjoy yourself."

They stood aside to let him pass. Bolan put the Saab in gear and accelerated out of there before they had a chance to change their minds. So far, so good. But they would certainly report his absence, if he had not been observed before he reached the gate.

The nearest town was Cashel, northeast along the coast. There would be pay phones, certainly, and even if IRA scouts spotted him in town, which struck him as a probability, at least he would have his conversation with Brognola.

The coastal highway was a narrow, winding, two-lane strip that would have been a single lane in any rural section of America. He hugged the low retaining wall at cliffside, taking full advantage of the straightaways to open up the Saab and take his portion from the middle of the road. The sea was on his left, a sparkling, restless vista stretching farther than the naked eye could see.

And Bolan could appreciate the beauty of it, but he was concentrating now on the ugly mission that had put him there. He knew that he had only scratched the surface with Binaggio and Esquilante. There was so much more to do and so little time.

He rounded one more curve, and suddenly the village was upon him, shops and houses crouching on the landward shoulder of the road. A more distracted driver might have passed it by without a sidelong glance, confused perhaps by momentary images reflected in the rearview mirror, quickly vanishing around another curve. He slowed the Saab and turned around outside a tiny general store, returning to the phone booth he had already passed.

The booths in Ireland were exactly that—no plastic bubbles—and all of them seemed freshly painted in a bright, eye-grabbing red. At home one would have been mistaken for a fire department call box, or perhaps an antique taxi stand.

He parked beside the booth and killed the Saab, delaying for a moment while he scanned the street in each direction, looking for familiar faces, anyone at all who seemed to take an interest in his presence. The street was empty, save for two old men reclining on a bench outside the general store, and neither one of them had found him worth a second glance. If there were scouts in Cashel, they were undercover.

He shut himself inside the booth and lifted the receiver. If his enemies were watching, they could take him here, boxed in, deprived of any combat stretch. It wouldn't be the first time that a phone booth doubled for a coffin. A sniper, stationed anywhere along the street, could pick him off before he finished dialing. A lorry, trundling along the road to market, passing through, could swerve up on the sidewalk and flatten Bolan, booth and all, before he had a chance to scramble clear.

He smiled, rejecting each scenario in turn as something from a cut-rate gangster film. If hunters were watching him, they would not risk an ambush in the middle of the tiny town. It would be so much cleaner, easier, to take him out at Cashel House, where he would be a sitting duck.

Except that Bolan was not sitting still for anyone this time. His war was going forward, and anyone who stood before the juggernaut had better be prepared to run or die.

Among the pocket litter he had lifted from The Face, there was a new phone company credit card. He rattled off the number and waited while the overseas operator confirmed it, repeating the number in Washington, D.C.

Allowing for the difference in time, it would be pushing 2:00 A.M. in Wonderland, and Bolan smiled, imagining the big, gruff fed asleep.

Brognola caught it on the second ring, his reflex right on time, but there was sleep behind the strong, familiar voice.

"Hello?" His tone spoke volumes. This had better be important.

"Good morning."

"It's good *night,*" the fed corrected him, "and who the hell . . ."

He was awake now, as he recognized the old, familiar voice.

"What time have *you* got?" he inquired.

"It's getting on toward lunch."

"I was afraid of that."

"Don't worry, I'm buying."

"I hope you can afford the tab."

Mack Bolan frowned. "It's higher than you know."

"How's that?"

"They're serving caviar and vodka now."

A momentary silence on the other end while Hal assimilated that, and when he spoke again his voice was hushed, intense. "Aw, shit."

"My sentiments, exactly."

"Any other innovations on the menu?"

"It's pretty much across the board. A lot of pasta, with some Asian appetizers on the side. They've got a Cuban entrée that I'd like to try."

"Be careful, huh? It might be hotter than you think."

"I'm counting on it."

"Yeah, I know."

There was concern in Hal Brognola's voice beneath the gruff exterior. He cared, damn right, and never mind that he could not afford to let it show.

"I guess you heard about our friend? The Reverend?"

"Mr. Black?"

"That's him. He had a little accident in his Manhattan apartment."

Alarm bells screamed in Bolan's head.

"Has next of kin been notified?"

"It's funny, there was some damned mix-up at the morgue, or something. Anyway, they *mis*identified the body, and the family hasn't claimed it yet."

A sudden surge of sweet relief for Bolan there, inside the close confinement of the booth. "Well, that's a shame," he said.

"You can't rely on anything these days."

"I'm learning that."

"So, when can we expect you home?"

"It's hard to say. I'm making lots of new friends here." He hesitated, knowing there would never be a better time, and finally forged ahead. "I've met a woman."

Surprise in Hal Brognola's voice. "Oh, yeah? Would it be anyone I know?"

"I couldn't say. She came in with the caviar."

"Uh-huh."

Another momentary silence on the line, and when Brognola spoke again, there was a different kind of urgency in his voice.

"You might be careful there," he said. "If she's the one I'm thinking of, her father in St. Cloud is very jealous of his girls."

The Executioner was instantly alert. St. Cloud, a Paris suburb, housed the central core of the international police network that coordinated operations all around the world.

"You figure she's a working girl?"

"I wouldn't know firsthand, but there are rumors, yeah."

"I see."

The presence of an agent at the conference did not surprise him now. In fact, he was expecting something of the sort. But he had not suspected Bridget Chambers—not of that, at any rate.

"I wouldn't dance too close," Brognola told him through the whisper static of the line. "She might be going steady there, or even setting up the party for a crash."

The Executioner was well ahead of him by now, extrapolating risks and calculating odds to fit the new equation.

"I have to stick," he told the worried fed. "It's on the line."

"Across the line, you mean. I know you too damn well—"

"So save us both some time," the soldier interrupted gently. "They'll be expecting me."

"Goddammit!"

Right.

And Bolan knew the feeling, the hopeless anger that developed when a friend was going in with everything he had, and there was nothing in the world that you could do to help bring him out again intact.

"It might not be that bad."

"My ass."

Brognola *knew* it would be bad. The worst, if the assembled powerhouses of the underworld were any indication.

"Well—"

"The kid says 'Hi.'"

The "kid" was Bolan's brother, Johnny, a man now, bloodied in the military and in Bolan's semiprivate war. He would be waiting at the San Diego Strongbase, monitoring telephone and radio, just waiting for the word.

"I'll be home when I can."

"He knows that, guy. We all know that."

It was time to break it off.

"They're holding lunch," Bolan said. "I wouldn't want to keep them waiting."

"Sure. And say, go easy on the caviar, all right?"

"I always clean my plate."

"Well, then, *bon appétit*."

The fragile link was broken, and he cradled the receiver slowly, conscious that the act was severing his only link with home.

If Bridget Chambers worked for Interpol, it put a new perspective on her presence at the meeting, on her search of Bolan's room—on everything, in fact. If she was setting up a raid, as Hal had hinted on the phone...

The reasonable thing to do was walk away, and leave the lady to her games. He could be back in Shannon by the afternoon, trading in his ticket for the first standby flight back to the United States.

It was the reasonable thing, damn right. But Bolan's private war had never been a reasonable conflict. It was touch and go, against the odds, against the dictates of a reasonable mind. The soldier couldn't win. He couldn't hope to stay alive, with all the savages arrayed against him in a grim, united front. It was unreasonable, sure.

And Bolan didn't give a damn.

If men were reasonable in their dealings with each other, war would not exist, his enemies would not exist. But since they did, since war was flesh-and-blood reality, the Executioner could not afford to turn his back and walk away, pretending blindness to the threat they posed. He was ready to communicate with his opponents in the only language they understood.

The dialect of thunder, pain and cleansing fire. Damn right.

He put the booth behind him, fired the Saab's impressive mill and powered out of Cashel, heading south and east along the coast toward the lodge.

A Fiat four-door passed him at the village outskirts, and he noted five men crammed inside the little car. His curiosity aroused, he tracked them in the rearview mirror, watching as the brake lights flared. The driver brought his wheels around outside the general store. Five faces, straining for a look at Bolan's Saab, and now the car was closing, eating up his lead. He saw the muzzle of a weapon poking up above the Fiat's dashboard, hastily withdrawn.

They were coming after Mack Bolan.

12

The winding coastal road had not been designed with speed in mind, but circumstances left the Executioner no choice. He floored the Saab's accelerator, keeping both hands on the wheel and clinging to the left-hand shoulder of the road, to reduce drifting on the curves. Although the chances were remote, he might meet other cars head-on at any time, and there would be no safety margin here, no room for error in his race with death.

Behind him, hanging close, the Fiat's driver was to provide his gunners with an angle of attack. Their weapons were apparent now, the muzzles poking out of open windows as they trailed the Executioner by several lengths. The convolutions of the road prevented them from taking aim, but they were hanging in there, waiting for the straightaway.

Bolan wondered if he had been observed by someone in the village, someone overlooked when he had scanned the street. If his departure from the lodge had triggered this reaction, that was something else entirely. That made it personal. But death was always personal in Bolan's world.

The Executioner was not prepared to end it here, and so he pushed the rental to its limit to prevent his enemy from pulling up beside him for a broadside fusillade. The Fiat's driver seemed experienced with Irish roads, or this road in particular. Repeatedly, he ran in close on Bolan's tail, maneuvering to pass, his gunners straining for a shot. Each time, Bolan milked another morsel of acceleration from the Saab, allowed its stern to drift, however slightly, cutting off the other lane.

It was a risky game, and both of them would eat it if they met another car approaching from the south. The warrior braced himself, prepared on every blind corner for the rush of pure adrenaline, the heartbeat warning before a crash.

It could go either way, of course. If he was not obliterated in a head-on crash, he might be driven inland, crushed against the hillside on his left. Survival would be fifty-fifty there, but if the crash car's driver panicked and swerved across his lane, the Saab would be deflected toward the cliff, the sea and certain death.

In that event Mack Bolan was determined that the Fiat would be going with him.

He concentrated on the road ahead. His danger lay behind him at the moment, and the threat of other motorists could be confronted when—and if—it came. The point was academic, anyway, if Bolan gave those hungry guns a chance to rake the Saab and blow him off the road.

But they were gaining, and he had it to the floorboard now, already pushing the machine beyond its limit on the narrow, winding road. The tires were screaming out on every curve, and Bolan fought the gears to keep the engine humping, knowing that if it stalled he was dead.

He needed some room to run, and Bolan's mind was racing, searching for an answer, when the Fiat's driver tried to pass again. The soldier cranked the steering wheel hard right, cutting the Saab across his enemy's path, his right rear fender and the corner of his bumper jostling the Fiat's nose.

He rode out the grinding impact, accelerating smoothly, one eye on the rearview mirror as he covered ground. The driver of the Fiat had been shaken; he was fighting for control, the little import drifting, swerving toward the cliff's edge and the sea below. They saved it at the final instant, but the Fiat's engine sputtered and stalled.

There had been no question of attempting to outrun the Fiat gunners, leading them to Cashel House and their employer's open arms. Bolan didn't know who set the crew against him, but his odds would be improved dramatically if he came home alone. The absence of pursuers would inspire confusion at the very least, and he could scan the faces, watching for a sign that anyone was worried, angry or surprised to see him.

They would have the Fiat running now, no doubt, and Bolan still had not picked out the perfect corner for his ambush. Never mind. When time was of the essence, savvy soldiers learn to compromise.

Another turn, a straightaway, and Bolan saw his chance. He braked and brought the Saab around until it sat across both lanes, a roadblock thirty yards beyond the nearest curve. Ahead of him the coastal road was flat and empty, lifeless under the noonday sun. Behind him he could almost see the hastening pursuit car, taking chances on the curves now, desperate to make up time.

He left the motor running, put the Saab in neutral, left his door wide open as he exited the car. The Beretta filled his hand and Bolan double-checked its load, then crouched behind the left-hand fender, pistol braced across the vehicle's hood.

Bolan heard the whining engine sounds an instant before seeing the enemy. They cleared the final corner in a slide, correcting violently, accelerating as the driver recognized the stretch of open road ahead, and braking suddenly, disastrously, as all eyes focused on the roadblock in their path.

It was a miracle they didn't roll, considering their speed, the way the driver locked his brakes and cut the wheel hard left without a moment's hesitation. They were sliding, rubber smoking on the road, and coming toward him broadside.

Bolan stroked a silent double-punch from the Beretta, holding steady on the mark, his empty casings bouncing across the hood of the Saab. He saw the Fiat's windshield sprout holes, the driver's face a screaming, crimson mask. Then, the wheelman lost it all. His lifeless hands were frozen on the steering wheel, his feet entangled with the brake and the accelerator, gunning the Fiat with his dying reflex. The little four-door surged ahead, nosed into the embankment and began to climb, defying gravity and losing out at last. The engine stalled again, and the Fiat slid backward and grumbled to a halt across both lanes.

The doors sprang open and the four surviving gunners laid down a screen of fire from automatic weapons as they scrambled for cover. Bolan's Saab was taking hits, the impact ringing in his ears. The bullet holes would call for some explaining when he returned to Cashel House.

If he returned.

The shotgun rider was compelled to exit under fire on Bolan's side, the alternate retreat cut off by his companion, who was draped across the steering wheel and leaking blood from ragged facial wounds. The gunner came out firing, ripping off a burst from his Beretta submachine gun.

Crouched behind the Saab, Bolan had his autoloader locked on target acquisition by the time his adversary hit the tarmac, crabbing sideways toward the inland shoulder of the road and the prospective cover of the Fiat's engine block. He stroked the trigger once, again. It was virtually impossible to miss at such close range.

The parabellum manglers lifted his assailant, punched him backward in an awkward sprawl across the Fiat's hood. The submachine gun clattered to the pavement as a final spasm racked the gunner's heavy frame, and then he lay still, draped across the fender like an outlandish hunting trophy.

His companions had unloaded on the other side, the Fiat blocking Bolan's line of fire, and their probing bursts of fire rattled through the Saab or gouged up divots in the asphalt underneath. They might get lucky any moment now, a stray round seeking out his fuel supply and striking sparks, the conflagration spreading to consume him—if the Executioner did not get lucky first.

He set the 93-R's fire-selector switch for 3-round bursts and braced himself, aware that he was risking everything right here, right now, on what amounted to a desperation play.

The soldier moved, erupting out of cover with the pistol braced in front of him at full arm's length, already sighting down the slide. He did not try to snipe the bobbing faces of his enemies as they recoiled with parting shots. His target was the car itself: the fuel line, carburetor, gas tank—any point where he could find a hot spot and fan it into open flame.

He stroked the sleek Beretta's trigger again and again, the short bursts rippling the muscles of his forearms, threatening to force the muzzle up and out of line. And still he held it firm, firing at the hostile car, until the slide locked open on an empty chamber.

But he had found his hot spot.

Smoke was curling up from beneath the Fiat's hood, pursued by licking flame, and gasoline was puddling beneath its rear axle. He crouched beneath a rain of cover fire, extracting a replacement magazine from underneath his arm and priming the Beretta for another round.

He could smell the burning fuel from where he crouched behind the Saab. Someone shouted a warning from the hostile camp.

The explosion rocked him, pushing angry shock waves across the highway. An oily ball of flame devoured the Fiat where it sat.

Bolan heard the gunners screaming, the panicked sound of tortured souls. He came erect, his pistol tracking, searching for a target. He did not have to wait long.

And a "dead" man was rising, a dancing human torch, bursting through a pall of greasy smoke to writhe at center stage. Bolan led his target, squeezed the trigger once and put a mercy round between the blackened, screaming lips. His target staggered, sprawled and smoldered in the middle of the road.

A second burning dervish came at Bolan from the other side, his tattered coat in flames. But this one had his wits about him, and he came at Bolan firing from the hip, his Uzi ripping off staccato bursts at thirty yards. A sidestep, parabellums crunching through the windshield of the Saab, and Bolan shot him twice before the gunner could correct his aim. The impact spun him half around; he was still firing as he fell, the Uzi emptying its load at sea and sky.

Four down, and that left only one alive, invisible behind the pall of smoke, the leaping flames. The Executioner would have to root him out. He meant to clean the slate with this one, and dispatch a message to the man behind the scenes, whoever he might be.

Emerging from the cover of the Saab, he listened for the slightest sound or movement that would give away his enemy. It was entirely possible the guy was dead, incinerated when the Fiat blew, but Bolan wasn't taking any chances this close to the finish line.

A scrabbling movement on his right alerted Bolan, and he swung around. His battered adversary was a sitting duck, perched halfway up the steep embankment, scrambling on his hands and knees to find a better vantage point. The grim expression on his bloody face revealed an understanding that the game was over now.

The gunner had an automatic tucked inside his waistband, and he tried to reach it but lost his footing, slipped and sat down hard. The piece was in his hand and he was grappling with the safety when a parabellum round exploded in his face, disintegrating cartilage and drilling through to find the brain. He was sprawling, rolling back in the direction of the Fiat funeral pyre as Bolan turned away.

Five up, five down, and it was over, for now.

Incredibly, the rubber on his Saab was still intact despite the shattered windows and a score of bullet holes that gave the body the appearance of a colander. The rental car would roll, provided he could get it started.

Bolan slid behind the wheel and twisted the ignition key. The engine grumbled, caught and finally purred. Against all odds, it had escaped the fusillade unscathed. He offered up a thank-you to the universe, put the Saab in gear and began rolling toward Cashel House.

Whoever had attempted to dispose of him would be surprised to see him back, alive and in one piece. They would be suitably embarrassed by the loss inflicted, by the beating taken at his hands. Inevitably, they would have to try again, to pay him back and even up the score. If that went down at Cashel House, within the summit meet itself, it could be the break that he was looking for.

Bolan's enemy—or one of them, at any rate—was wounded now. That made him doubly dangerous. If five were not enough to take the Executioner, there might be ten next time, fifteen.

He didn't like the math in that equation, and he pushed it out of mind, concentrating on the other problem that was nagging for attention.

Bridget Chambers.

If she was Interpol, as Hal suggested on the phone, then she was one more obstacle in Bolan's path. He had no wish to throw her life away, but she was in the middle of the killing ground, attached to one of Bolan's leading targets, and she might not run for cover when the heat came down.

It troubled Bolan, as the presence of an uninvited comrade or an innocent civilian in the fire zone always troubled him. She would need looking after, and the mere distraction of her presence was enough to get him killed unless he exercised a special care.

So be it. She was in the game, and there was nothing he could do about it now. He would protect her if he could, but in the end his mission took priority, and they were both expendable. The lady would have known the dangers going in, and she would live or die, depending on how well she did her job.

For his part, Bolan recognized the task that lay ahead, and nothing short of death would hold him back. The two attempts upon his life were not discouraging. If anything, they told him he was getting close.

But close to what? To whom?

The answers waited for him back at Cashel House, and he accelerated now, the burning Fiat a dwindling smudge on the horizon. There was a serpent's nest awaiting him in paradise, down the winding coastal road, and Bolan meant to drive the human snakes out of old Ireland.

His plan was right on time so far. The gunners hadn't even slowed him down. If anything, the two attacks had strengthened his grim determination to succeed. The enemy had angered Bolan now, and once he passed inside the gates at Cashel House, they would have him surrounded.

God help them all.

13

The sentries were surprised and shaken by the bullet holes in Bolan's rented Saab. The taller one checked out the damage, while his partner strolled toward the tommy guns stashed inside the gate. His eyes were furtive, anxious, darting back and forth along the highway in search of enemies.

"It seems ye had some trouble, sir."

"You ought to see the other guy."

"I'll need to do jus' that."

Mack Bolan shrugged.

"You'll find them two clicks north, before you get to Cashel, if a wrecker hasn't hauled the mess away."

The sentry's eyebrow briefly climbed in the direction of his hairline, finally settled back in place.

"Survivors?"

"Not on their side, guy."

"An' did you recognize them, sir, by any chance?"

"No chance at all. I'd say they were recruited for a job they couldn't handle, and they blew it."

Bolan heard the static crackle of a radio, and glancing past the nearest IRA commando, spied his partner with a walkie-talkie, Thompson submachine gun tucked beneath his arm.

They were reporting, and Bolan had expected that. They would be checking out the wreckage he had left behind, to learn—or cover up—identities before police arrived.

He kept an eye on the commando with the Thompson, ready if the guy should make a hostile move, but there was nothing going down. Not here. Not now.

"I'd say that you were very lucky, sir."

"You make your own luck, fella. Don't forget it."

"Yessir. Mr. Scalish will be wantin' a word, when you've had time to freshen up a bit."

"That's good. I've got a word or two for him, about his hot security arrangements on this deal."

His words hit home, and the commando stiffened, color rising in his cheeks. He was about to answer, but he reconsidered, and stepped back from the Saab.

"Take care now, sir."

"I'm always careful," Bolan told him as he gunned the Saab along the driveway.

He stashed the ventilated rental in the parking lot and didn't bother locking it. There were no valuables inside, and anyone who wanted to could reach in through the shattered windshield, anyway. The car was a mess, but it would roll, and that was all he needed in a set of wheels.

To Bolan, the IRA commandos on the gate had registered sincere surprise at the attempt upon his life. They didn't measure up as Oscar candidates, by any means, and if they were forewarned of the attack, they hid it very well. The gunner with the walkie-talkie had been nervous— really nervous—when he made his call, and Bolan wondered just how much security there really was at Cashel House. If nothing else was clear, he realized that someone planned to guide the meeting, guarantee that everything turned out as planned.

Joe Scalish? Possibly.

Alexei Gladnikov? Another heavy possible.

Or someone else entirely?

Damn.

It was the unknown quantity that made Mack Bolan edgy now, his combat senses on alert as he walked back to the hotel. He checked in through the front this time, expecting Scalish to be waiting for him, primed for the interrogation like a vulture for the kill, but no one stopped him as he passed the dining room, the lounge and registration desk, proceeding on along the corridor until he reached his room.

He hesitated, with his key already in the lock, remembering the night before. If someone should be waiting for him inside, he did not plan to be taken by surprise. A final glance along the corridor both ways, and Bolan eased the 93-R from its shoulder rigging, flicked the safety off and cocked the hammer.

He turned the key and slipped inside. The door was not completely closed behind him when the soldier realized that he was not alone.

"Is that the way you always enter rooms?"

The lady had been waiting for him, and now she sat up in his bed, the sheets and bedspread slipping, saved before they passed the point of no return.

"It all depends," he answered, checking out the empty bathroom and holstering the automatic as he moved to stand beside the bed. "Some places, you can trust the locks."

"There's nothing wrong with these." Her smile was brilliant, dazzling. "Let's say that I'm determined."

"So I see."

"Truth is, I owe you thanks."

"How's that?"

"For not complaining to Alexei, telling him you caught me here."

He sat beside the bed and propped his feet up on the mattress, his ankles crossed. The lady didn't move; her coverlet, with the restraining hand removed, slipped downward a delicious half inch farther.

Bolan met the lady's steady gaze.

"He sent you in to check me out. If I have any gripes with that I'll take them out of his account, not yours."

She frowned, not quite a pout but close enough.

"That's just the point, you see. He didn't send me. Not exactly."

"Ah."

The soldier was enjoying her predicament. He meant to let her find the exit for herself.

"I mean that I was...interested...when I saw you in the dining room. I hoped that we could get to know each other, in the little time we have."

"So you searched my room."

Exasperation etched a pretty smile on Bridget Chambers's face.

"I've always been a cautious person, Mr. Black. I had to check you out, before..."

She left the sentence hanging there, unfinished, filled with latent promises.

"Your caution seems to be a little shaky," Bolan said. "That's twice I've caught you, now.

The smile was back, and Bridget shook her head.

"That's once. It doesn't count if I get caught deliberately."

"Okay. And where's Alexei hanging out while you play hide-and-seek?"

The lady tossed her head, the movement putting auburn waves in motion all around her face, across her naked shoulders.

"Busy with his meetings, naturally. I must say, I'm surprised you aren't involved."

"I took the morning off to do some shooting practice," Bolan told her casually. "Turns out somebody got me mixed up with the target."

"What?" Her attitude had changed, and something like concern was showing now, together with a healthy dose of pure surprise. "You mean that someone tried to kill you?"

Bolan shrugged.

"I didn't stop to check their hunting license. Anyway, we worked it out."

"They got away?"

"Not exactly."

It took a moment for the meaning of his words to register, and then the lady paled.

"Who were they?"

"I was hoping you could help me there."

"But how could I . . . you think . . . oh, no, it isn't possible. Alexei wouldn't take the chance. Not here, with everything at stake."

"Could be he's got too much at stake."

The lady shook her head. "I don't believe it. No, it must be someone else."

"I bow to your experience as a professional."

Her eyes were narrowed as she watched him. "Exactly what is that supposed to mean?"

He smiled disarmingly and glanced around the suite. "I hate a room with bugs, don't you? No telling where they'll hide, and creep up on you when you least expect it."

Bridget Chambers caught his meaning instantly this time, and she was frowning as she answered. "Speak your piece. It's clean. I checked for microphones last night, and then again this morning, just in case."

"I guess it's safety first at Interpol these days."

Her face went blank, as if the Executioner had slapped her hard across the cheek. It took a moment for her to regain her voice.

"There must be some misunderstanding here. I'm not—"

"From Interpol? I guess my sources had it wrong."

"What are your sources, Mr. Black?"

"So much formality. Why don't you call me Mike?"

"I'm listening."

Her voice was taut, impatient now, and there was more than just a trace of fear beneath the words.

"Relax. Your secret's safe with me."

"Assuming that I have a secret to protect, of course."

"Of course."

"Are you . . ."

"An agent?" Bolan shook his head. "Not even close. I've got some friends, who have some friends. That's all."

"But if you're not..." She hesitated, trying desperately to make the pieces fit and getting nowhere fast. At length she told the warrior, "I don't understand."

"You're not supposed to."

"What's your interest in Alexei Gladnikov?" she challenged him.

"I never heard the name before last night."

"Your interest in the meeting, then?"

"It's personal."

"Your invitation..."

"Borrowed from a friend. He didn't need it anymore."

"And you are not the man they think you are."

"I am, for now."

They stared at one another in uneasy silence, the tension drawn between them like a taut, steel spring.

"I guess you have that thank-you coming, after all," she said, "considering you could have had me killed."

"I know your secret, you know part of mine. I'd say that makes us even."

"Not just yet."

She shifted slightly in the bed, and gravity asserted its control upon the sheets and bedspread, pooling them around her waist. Her breasts, revealed to Bolan, were small, firm and perfectly proportioned.

The soldier felt himself responding, and he swallowed hard.

"This isn't necessary."

"Maybe not for you."

But it was definitely necessary for Bolan, too. The sudden urgency was like a thermite fire inside him, burning from the entrails out and melting his defenses in the process.

Most of his defenses, anyway.

He stipped, standing beside the bed, her eyes devouring his every movement. Then he reached down, tangled anxious fingers in the bedclothes, drew them back and let them fall away. The lady from Interpol lay where she was, allowing him to study her. When she reached for him, her fingers seared his flesh. She drew him down and folded him within herself, her legs a satin vise that locked around his hips.

Mack Bolan tucked the Beretta beneath a pillow, out of sight but still within his reach. Then he turned his full attention to the woman, at first matching her frenetic movements with his own, then slowly and deliberately easing the pace, taking time to savor each sensation individually.

She understood, and let herself go limp beneath him, her dark eyes open wide and staring at him, the silken fan of auburn hair spread out around her face. She started to accommodate his rhythm, thrusting gently, now with mounting urgency, her fingernails like talons, digging into his shoulders, raking at his naked back. She let him feel her secret strength, and laughed to see the sudden flush of color rising in his face.

The moment was too primal, too intense to last, and Bolan buried his face against the hollow of her throat. He heard her gasp, and now the sound was rising to a yelp, a scream. . . .

Except that Bridget's voice was muffled now, somehow, as if she had been calling to him from another room. The sound was strange, so far away.

Bolan pushed up on his elbows, met the lady's eyes— and knew at once the screaming voice did not belong to anyone inside his suite. It was outside, beyond the bedroom door, a rising, panicked note of someone shrieking in the corridor.

"Goddammit."

Right. He knew precisely how the lady felt.

Bolan leaped out of bed and reached for his slacks, the automatic pistol in his hand before he hit the floor. It was a rude awakening from Eden, sure, but then again the Executioner had turned his back on the garden long ago. He was committed to the firing line of here and now, damn right. He had no choice.

No choice at all.

14

Bolan burst into the hallway and found that others had arrived before him, answering the panicked screams. He recognized the Triad delegates, a couple of the Corsicans, the stick-together New York representatives.

Joe Scalish held a sobbing woman by the shoulders, bent down to whisper something, his lips pressed close against her ear. Whatever he was saying it was getting through, and Bolan could see that she was calming down, still weeping but in silence now.

He didn't recognize the woman, but her uniform and cleaning cart abandoned in the middle of the corridor identified her as a maid. She had been entering the suite, from all appearances, and Bolan saw the tall door standing open, surrounded by the growing crowd of gangland delegates. He shouldered past the men from Hong Kong, strained to get a look inside.

And found a body stretched out in the entrance.

The Colombian lay on his back, his dead eyes focused on the ceiling. His face was blank, impassive, but a ragged second mouth was grinning beneath his chin, esophagus and trachea exposed where they were severed by a single, sweeping cut. For emphasis, the killer had continued stabbing him, a dozen times or more, once he was down. The scattered, nearly bloodless rents in flesh and clothing told the Executioner that the Hispanic was dead before he hit the ground.

The other three Colombians arrived, attracted by the furor in the corridor. They formed a flying wedge to part the other delegates, and froze at the sight of their dead team member. It took a moment for the stunned surprise to pass, and then the three of them were shouting, cursing, arguing in Spanish, with themselves and with the mobsters gathered all around who could not understand a word.

Joe Scalish moved to intercept them on the threshold, and his eyes met Bolan's briefly, throwing sparks before they moved away. Bolan could sense that the New Yorker was under pressure, and this would not do anything to ease his load, unless, of course, he had arranged the hit himself.

The capo from Manhattan was cajoling, pleading with the Hispanic delegates to calm themselves, to answer him in English. They tried a few obscenities, then finally settled down to hear the capo's questions out.

From what the Executioner could gather, they were staring at the last remains of poor Ramon, a combination of altruist and altar boy who would, in time, have found his place among the saints. The fact that he was many times a murderer, that he was here at Cashel House to organize a major cocaine route, was not considered pertinent. The three Colombians had lost a friend, and they were scared. It showed in their excitement, in their agitated speech, their darting eyes.

And that was fine with Bolan. The more dissension that arose among the delegates, the easier his job would be. And if they started killing one another off that was fine, too.

He wondered if poor Ramon's demise could be related to his own attacks. It was a possibility, of course, and nothing could be arbitrarily dismissed so early in the game.

The three Colombians were arguing in heated terms with Scalish, expressing their contempt for him, for his security arrangements, for their fellow delegates in general.

DYNAMITE OFFER

4 EXPLOSIVE NOVELS
PLUS A QUARTZ WATCH
FREE

**delivered right to your home
with no obligation to buy—ever**

TAKE 'EM FREE

4 action-packed novels and a digital quartz watch

With an offer like this, how can you lose?

Return the attached card, and we'll send you 4 adventure novels just like the one you're reading plus a digital quartz calendar watch—ABSOLUTELY FREE.

If you like them, we'll send you 6 books every other month to preview. Always before they're available in stores. Always for less than the retail price. Always with the right to cancel and owe nothing.

NON-STOP HIGH-VOLTAGE ACTION

As a Gold Eagle subscriber, you'll get the fast-paced, hard-hitting action you crave. Razor-edge stories stripped to their lean muscular essentials. Written in a no-holds-barred style that keeps you riveted from cover to cover.

In addition you'll receive...

- our free newsletter AUTOMAG with every shipment

- special books to preview free and buy at a deep discount

RUSH YOUR ORDER TO US TODAY

Don't let this bargain get away. Send for your 4 free books and wristwatch now. They're yours to keep even if you never buy another Gold Eagle book.

Digital quartz watch keeps you right on time

Unbeatable! That's the word for this tough water-resistant timepiece. Easy-to-read LCD display beams exact time, date and running seconds with flawless quartz precision. Full one-year warranty (excluding battery).

FREE BOOKS & WATCH

YEAH, send my 4 **free** Gold Eagle novels plus my **free** watch. Then send me 6 brand-new Gold Eagle novels (2 **Mack Bolans** and one each of **Phoenix Force, Able Team, Track** and **SOBs**) every second month as they come off the presses. Bill me at the low price of $2.25 each (for a total of $13.50 per shipment—a saving of $1.50 off the retail price). There are no shipping, handling or other hidden charges. I can always return a shipment and cancel at any time. Even if I never buy a book from Gold Eagle, the 4 free books and the watch (a $29.95 value) are mine to keep.

166 CIM PAHT

Name	(PLEASE PRINT)

Address	Apt. No.

City	State/Prov.	Zip/Postal Code

Offer limited to one per household and not valid for present subscribers. Prices subject to change.

FREE

JOIN FORCES WITH GOLD EAGLE'S HEROES

- Mack Bolan...lone crusader against the Mafia and KGB
- Able Team...3-man combat squad blitzes global terrorism
- Phoenix Force...5 mercenaries battle international crime
- Track...weapons genius stalks madman around the world
- SOBs...avengers of justice from Vietnam to Iran

For free offer, detach and mail

"What kin'a hot security you call this, eh, *pendejo*?"

"What security? Where's all those *hombres machos* we were promised?"

Scalish raised his hands, and none too soon. Already there were quiet grumblings among the other delegates in the corridor. Another moment and the New York capo could be looking at a minirevolution in the ranks. He had to get the lid on now before the whole thing fell apart.

"If we could have it quiet, please. You all were guaranteed security, and that's exactly what we've got."

A rising undertone of muttered threats and accusations, with the tallest of the three Colombians confronting Scalish face-to-face.

"So maybe you can tell us how Ramon got killed, if your security is so damn tight?"

Scalish stiffened, frowned.

"One thing's for sure, he wasn't iced by anyone from outside this hotel."

A momentary silence, then the delegates exploded, crowding close, demanding explanations, clearly frightened that they understood the mafioso only too well.

"I'm saying that the grounds are sealed off tight," Joe Scalish answered, shouting to be heard above the din. "Nobody got in here to kill this man an' then got out again. It's just impossible."

The tall Colombian stepped back, glancing at the solemn faces ringed about him.

"You mean somebody here has done this thing? One of your delegates?"

The Manhattan mobster spread his hands. "Who knows why these things happen, eh? A grudge from years ago, or maybe someone wants a bigger slice of pie."

All three Colombians were shouting now. They understood the accusation plain enough, in any tongue, and they were not disposed to take it lying down. The others closed around them, waiting for the outburst to exhaust itself, and then Joe Scalish held the floor again.

"I'm not attaching blame to anybody here," he said, in soothing tones. "What's done is done. We can't bring back the dead. Now, I can shut the conference down, and we can spend the weekend looking for a killer that we'll prob'ly never find. Or we can all get back to business, and start making money. What'll it be?"

They were listening now, the members of different delegations whispering and nodding among themselves. Even the Colombians seemed to be relaxing slightly, taking the edge off.

"We can't go home with poor Ramon this way," their spokesman said at last.

Joe Scalish nodded understanding at their plight.

"I'll get a couple fellas on it right away. The garden's nice this time of year. You want, we can throw in a little service for your friend."

The tall Colombian glanced left and right at his companions, finally shook his head.

"*No es necesario.* The sooner we get down to business, the sooner we can all go home."

"My sentiments, exactly," Scalish beamed.

He had pulled it off. The New York mafioso had succeeded in defusing an explosive situation. Bolan didn't have the first idea of who had iced the dead Colombian, but it presented him with some attractive possibilities. Another death or two might rattle Scalish just enough to make him lose control. And if a number of the delegates were on their guard already, helped along by cautious words from Mr. Black . . .

You could have cut the paranoia with a knife as members of the delegations returned to their suites. Bolan watched Scalish for a moment, sizing up his target, letting Scalish notice him, the sleek Beretta in his hand. It was enough for now, and Bolan wore a smile of satisfaction as he returned to his room.

A smile that vanished as he discovered that the lady had evaporated from the scene. She was gone, without a trace.

SHE HAD STAYED IN BED for several moments after "Michael Black" had scrambled clear, responding to the sound of screaming from the corridor. A maelstrom of confused sensations and emotions seemed to hold her paralyzed, but Bridget Chambers finally shook them off and threw the covers back, scooping up her clothes and dressing swiftly as she heard angry voices outside.

She was professional enough to keep her wits about her, even in the heat of passion.

The man had known she was Interpol. Somehow, impossibly, the stranger knew.

And he was not the man she had expected, either. He was clearly not The Face, whoever else he might turn out to be.

The problem would be finding out precisely who he was, and how he knew so much about her undercover role. If he could break down her cover so easily, Alexei might be next, and Bridget didn't even want to think about the consequences that would carry. If the Russian thought that she was anything but loyal, obedient . . .

A shudder raced along her spine, unrelated to the tingling in her limbs, her body, which the stranger had so recently inspired. She had intended to seduce him in the line of duty, to secure information toward completion of her case, but it had turned into another sort of contact altogether. He had broken through her cool reserve as no man had in years, and now that he was gone, distracted prematurely by the action in the corridor, she felt frustrated.

She finished dressing and pushed the carnal memories away. Before she tried to crack the mystery of Michael Black, before she could continue with her job, she had to put this room behind her, undetected. If Alexei learned that she had been here, let alone gone to bed with someone he regarded as the competition, her cover would be blown beyond recovery. And with her cover gone she was as good as dead.

The stranger hadn't tipped Alexei to their first encounter, that was obvious. Whatever private motives kept him silent, she was grateful, but her problem was the here and now. Outside, the corridor was filled with angry, shouting men. Alexei might be with them, or on his way. In any case, it would be difficult for her to clear the suite and make it back to Gladnikov's room undetected.

Difficult, but not impossible.

But no matter what the odds, she had to try.

A backward glance in the direction of the rumpled bed, a surge of primal heat that left her giddy for an instant, was swiftly gone, and she was on her way. She reached the door and hesitated, listening to frightened, angry voices somewhere on her right, perhaps two doors away.

From what she overheard, it seemed that someone, one of the Colombians, was dead. The New York gangster, Scalish, was attempting to restore some order, offering assurances about security and protection for the other delegates, and he was facing opposition all the way. With luck, he might command their full attention long enough for Bridget to complete her exit unnoticed.

She could picture the hallway clearly, curving to the right as it approached the stairs, the registration office and the dining room beyond. She didn't have to get that far; her target was a doorway that led to the garden in the rear. From there she could reenter the hotel from any one of several doors, and explain to Gladnikov, if he should ask, that she had been walking in the garden.

If she was not observed emerging from the stranger's room.

No time for hesitation now. She braced herself, threw back the door, stepped through and into the corridor. The voices seemed to leap at her, but when she glanced to her right, the crowd was still beyond her line of sight, around the corner of the hallway. She would cross their field of vision momentarily before she reached the outer door, but if she kept her wits about her, if she slipped out quickly enough . . .

Half a dozen strides were all it took to reach the door. The lady did not look around to see if anyone had noticed her, although she knew that they could see her now, if anybody cared to glance her way. She prayed that they were all distracted by the dead man, by their fear of being next or by their anger at the failure of security.

The door swung shut behind her, and the lady operative let her pent-up breath escape between clenched teeth. The midday sun was warm and welcome, bringing out the fragrance of the grass beneath her feet, the ferns and flowers of the gardens where they crept up close upon the flank of the hotel.

She let herself relax, reverting to a casual stroller's attitude as she began to work her way around the rear of the hotel. No point in rushing and drawing more attention to herself. If Gladnikov should find her now, she had been walking, killing time and nothing more. The questions that filled Bridget's mind were not reflected on her smiling face.

But most of them were about Michael Black, this stranger who had altered everything, disturbed the whole equation of her mission here at Cashel House. She wondered who he was and what had brought him to this place. He might be CIA, of course, or even FBI.

She felt another chill despite the sunlight's radiating warmth, but it was not unpleasant. She would be back with Gladnikov before another hour passed, and when the evening sessions were completed, he would call for her, as always. This time, though, she would not have to make her mind a blank, to suffer through the ordeal with a plastic smile on her face.

This time, when she was in Alexei's bed, she would be thinking of the stranger, Michael Black, and living through their brief encounter of the afternoon. It was enough for now. Tomorrow was another day with pain and pleasures of its own.

THE JOB HAD NOT APPEALED to Seamus Kelly from the start. He was a soldier and a revolutionary, not a bodyguard. He should have been in Ulster, fighting in the streets, directing moves against the British occupation troops instead of playing nursemaid to the gangster scum collected here. He had no more in common with the lot than with the gang at Downing Street.

Then again, he had accepted the assignment as a favor to the Russian, Gladnikov, and he would be repaid if all went well. They had done business in the past, for weapons, ammunition and explosives. Generous and accommodating, Gladnikov seemed to understand the Irish revolution in a way so few outsiders ever could. He spoke of revolution in his native country, and the suffering that had preceded victory, the blood required to wash away injustice and iniquity.

It was a sham, of course, and Seamus Kelly knew it. Gladnikov was under orders from the KGB to lend a hand with any revolution, anywhere, dispensing weapons, funds and "free" advice that always seemed to come with strings attached. In recent years, Gladnikov had lavished his largesse upon the Red Brigades, the Baader-Meinhof gang, the South Moluccans and the Basque ETA commandos in the Pyrenees. His interest in the Irish struggle was pragmatic, mercenary and undoubtedly dictated from above.

But he was useful all the same, especially in these days when aid from the United States was being interdicted more efficiently by agents of the FBI and Garda troops at home. The flow of cash and arms from overseas was dwindling, and Kelly knew that he would have to bargain with the devil, if it came to that, where weapons were concerned.

The Cashel House assignment was a simple job, according to Alexei's estimate. A group of foreign "businessmen," obsessed with privacy, were gathering to hammer out a worldwide coalition of their kind. They would be willing to employ a paramilitary force at top rates to guarantee that they were undisturbed.

A simple job, remote from all the perils of the North. A virtual vacation.

Except that now, the "businessmen" had been disturbed, and one of them was lying dead inside his suite. It mattered little that his killer must have come from the inside, as Scalish said. Security had failed, and Kelly would be held accountable.

He was relieved that Gladnikov had not responded to the shrieking of the maid. There would be time to reach him before others filled his head with images of random killers roaming through the hills. It would be impossible to reason with him, keep the incident from being blown out of proportion.

Kelly was already turning from the crowd of delegates, intent on being first to greet Alexei with the news, when furtive movement filled the corner of his eye. He hesitated, turned—and froze at the sight of Gladnikov's companion, Bridget Chambers, slinking through a side door, out into the garden behind the hotel.

The IRA commander frowned, pondering the questions that her presence here, away from Gladnikov, had brought to mind. How many suites remained along the short length of the corridor? He visualized the floor plan in his head and counted two. The farthest from the point at which he stood was occupied by the Vietnamese, and Kelly knew that they were in the conference room, or had been moments earlier, still making plans with Gladnikov. The nearest of the two belonged to... whom?

Bare-chested and barefoot, the tall American who had been registered as Michael Black was standing on the fringe of the excited little crowd, a semiautomatic pistol in his hand. The weapon came as no surprise to Kelly; he had already received the news about an ambush on the highway north of the hotel. It was the stateside mobster's attitude, his lack of clothing, that was setting off the warning bells in Kelly's mind.

Bridget Chambers had been with him in his room.

The IRA commander smiled as he recognized the implications. He realized he had something that he could trade with Gladnikov. The Russian would be furious about the death of the Colombian, providing that he had not set it up himself, and it would make no difference that the killer must be one of the surviving delegates. Kelly had failed to prevent the murder of a man he had been hired to protect.

But now, with Bridget's secret in his hands, there would be something he could offer Gladnikov, a bit of news the Russian couldn't get by huddling with his friends, the Cubans and Vietnamese. Before he got wound up and started raving in his native tongue, the Irishman would hit him where it hurt and leave him wondering precisely what the woman might be up to once she slipped out of his sight.

It was a small bit of leverage, but Kelly needed all he could get. It just might be enough to turn the heat away from his commandos or from himself.

Providing he could reach the Russian first and break the news *his* way. The Irishman was smiling as he left Joe Scalish to pacify the crowd. As master of ceremonies of the convention, it was his duty, after all.

And Seamus Kelly had a duty of his own this afternoon. Self-preservation.

15

Alexei Gladnikov enjoyed the taste of Irish whiskey. Sweeter than the vodka of his native land, it warmed a man inside without simultaneously embalming him. There was something mellow in the amber liquid, something that eluded the distillers back in Mother Russia. If it hadn't been so counter-revolutionary an idea, he might have taken home a sample, with suggestions that they overhaul the ancient recipe.

The others had been watching him as he enjoyed his drink. Alexei felt their eyes upon him and he smiled, aware that they must think him absentminded, even senile, to let a glass of whiskey so distract him from the task at hand.

But Gladnikov was far from senile. He was as absentminded as a calculator when it came to doing business with the likes of the Vietnamese and Cubans who were grouped around his table.

The KGB did not put senile agents in the field. It put them out to pasture, figuratively—and sometimes literally.

Gladnikov was perfectly aware of the inquiring eyes around him, the anxiety behind those eyes, as he placed his glass of whiskey on the polished table top. He half-turned to face the frowning Cuban on his left.

"I understand your personal misgivings, Esteban. As you must understand our larger goal, the greater need."

The Cuban made a sour face. "To deal with these ... these *hijos de*—"

Alexei raised a hand to cut him off. "Your history is known to me. I realize that men like these once occupied Havana, when the pig, Batista, was in power." Gladnikov allowed himself a little smile. "But things are different now, *amigo*. It is they who come to you, with hats in hand, to curry favor from Fidel."

"They come with hats in hand and knives behind their backs," the Cuban grumbled. "I will never trust these *animales*."

"Nor shall I," the Russian readily agreed. "But we can use them, all the same. If they believe that they are in control..."

He left the statement hanging there, but the Cuban understood. He nodded grudgingly, but he was far from pacified.

"We have been dealing with these men for over thirty years," a slim Vietnamese remarked to no one in particular. "Their money helps support our revolution, and the poison they dispense has sapped our enemies of their vitality, their strength. The poppy is a better weapon than the rifle, Esteban, if used with skill."

"*Comprendo, sí*. But it is not so easy to forgive."

"Forgive them nothing," Gladnikov replied, his gray eyes cold and hard as slate. "When we are finished with this scum, when they have served us, we will deal with them from strength. For now, they dominate the markets that we need. They are a way inside our common enemy's defenses, Esteban. We need them now. But later...."

"*Sí*. I will be looking forward to the later with anticipation."

Seamus Kelly was walking across the dining room at an urgent pace. He was frowning; but then again he seldom smiled. Gladnikov decided he would find out precisely what the IRA commander wanted, before he started worrying.

Arriving at the table, Kelly smiled briskly, politely. His eyes were riveted upon the Russian's face.

"We need to have a word," he said, his tone informing Gladnikov that they should have the word alone.

The man from Russia excused himself from his companions, acutely conscious of the anger on the Cuban's face. It was the slick Vietnamese, however, who concerned him more. The Asian really was inscrutable, in all the ways that counted, and Alexei Gladnikov could not escape a feeling that the Hanoi delegate might have an ace or two concealed inside his sleeve.

When they had moved some distance from the table, Gladnikov confronted Kelly, tempered steel beneath the velvet of his voice.

"I trust this is a matter of importance."

"I'm inclined to think so," Kelly told him. "Someone just removed one-fourth of the Colombian contingent. All the way."

The Russian stiffened, fought to keep surprise from showing on his face.

"Which one?"

"Montoya, I believe. His friends were calling him Ramon."

"What happened?"

Kelly shrugged, a casual rolling of his massive shoulders that revealed the power hidden there.

"An inside job," he said. "We know that much. No strangers on the grounds."

"You're sure?"

The Irishman responded with a condescending sigh. "My men are on the job. The only person in or out so far today was the American, that Michael Black."

Alexei Gladnikov was frowning, struggling to make the pieces fit, by force if necessary. "Any more about that other incident?"

The IRA commander shook his head. "It's with the Garda, now. The bodies either burned, or else they hadn't any papers. Fingerprints will take some time, if they come up with anything at all."

"And the police?"

"They're curious enough, but there's nothing to connect that lot with Cashel House."

"The curiosity is something I can live without."

"It's nothing," Kelly told him, sounding confident. "Unless, of course, the car checks back to someone here."

"Are you suggesting a connection with Montoya?"

Kelly shrugged again, and tucked both hands inside his pockets.

"It's a thought. Supposing the Colombians had somethin' in for Black, a grudge, say. They try to take him out, they miss, and Black comes home to even up the score a bit."

The Russian chewed it over, pondering the possibilities. "You may be right. And then again..."

"Third parties?"

"It's a possibility."

"We'll check it out."

"May I assume—"

"I'm doubling security," the Irishman responded, cutting off the question. "No one leaves from here on out unless he takes an escort with him."

"Excellent. And what about interior?"

"I'm bringing half a dozen men inside. They'll be rigged out as waiters, somethin' of the sort, an' they'll be handy if there's any further row."

"I leave it in your hands," the Russian said, turning to go.

"There's one thing more," said the Irishman.

"Go on."

"The woman."

"What?"

"The woman in your party. Bridget Chambers, is it?"

Gladnikov looked closely at the Irishman, scrutinizing him.

"That is correct."

His voice was wary now, and he could feel the sudden tension, prickling like a rash between his shoulder blades. One fist was tightly clenched against his thigh, the whitened knuckles pressing hard against his leg.

"It may be none of my concern, but—"

"Get on with it!"

"When I was checking on Montoya, I observed her in the corridor."

Alexei's eyebrows met above his nose, and there was something dangerous behind his eyes.

"So?"

"The thing is, sir, that it struck me odd, her comin' from the direction that she did."

His voice devoid of all expression, the Russian prompted Kelly to continue.

"What direction, Kelly?"

"Why, from his room, sir. That Michael Black."

The prickling was back, but Gladnikov relaxed his fist, allowed the fabric of his slacks to blot the sudden perspiration from his palm.

"Perhaps you knew already, sir?"

"I'll handle it," the Russian told his captain of security.

"Of course."

"As for the other matters we discussed—"

"They're taken care of, sir."

"All right. And thank you, Kelly."

"Pleasure, sir."

He meant it, and the Russian cursed him silently as he returned to join his Cuban and Vietnamese associates. They had been watching the exchange from a distance, and they would be expecting to be enlightened. It was their due.

But he would tell them only what he felt they had to know. The woman was a private problem, one he could handle on his own, without advice or interference from a group of cut-rate Third World warlords.

He would enlighten them no more than necessary, and they had no need to know about the girl. She was Alexei's problem, and he was mentally plotting solutions even as he took his seat.

Perhaps the girl was simply attracted to this brash American, excited by his rugged looks and violent lifestyle. Gladnikov had never gone so far as to delude himself that she was with him out of love. His money kept her loyal, but when the flesh came into play would her loyalty shift?

Perhaps there was more than casual sex behind their meeting. The possibility gave Alexei pause. He could dismiss a minor infidelity without a second thought; he, himself, had not been faithful to her, either. But what if she had betrayed him in some other way?

Was Bridget in league against him? He would require more proof than Kelly's unsupported word, of course. The Irishman was on his payroll, and they had worked together before, but Kelly had a way of looking through Gladnikov and picking out the mercenary aspects of his soul. They neither liked each other nor trusted each other much beyond the basic deals for arms and explosives, which the IRA required to prosecute its Ulster war. The Russian knew that Kelly wouldn't lie in such a blatant way, and yet, what had he really seen?

The only person who could answer those and all the other nagging questions would be waiting for Alexei in his suite. She would resist, of course. He knew her well enough to know that it would not be easy. But eventually, he would break her down.

Another sip of Irish whiskey, and the Russian found that he was eagerly anticipating the confrontation, as a child awaits his birthday, anxious to unwrap his toys. It would be exciting to explore her in a new and different way, to find the essence of her fear, her weakness and employ that secret knowledge to possess her totally, once and for all.

As Alexei Gladnikov turned to the Cuban and the Vietnamese delegates at his table, there were traces of a smirk at the edges of his mouth.

16

Henri Bouchet was frequently obsessed with the idea of growing old. He had already spent a lifetime in his present trade, and there was little consolation that it fell just short of thirty-seven years. By any actuarial accounting, he was halfway to the grave, and he was feeling more depressed about his age with every passing day.

The Corsican did not aspire to immortality. He had rejected God and the church when he was old enough to run the streets and learn a new religion for himself. He worshiped power now, the awe that fear and wealth inspired in lesser men and women. Ah, the women...

But it was the power that intrigued Bouchet. Already a man of some authority in his native land, he wanted to expand his realm, create an empire for himself that would transcend the flesh and make him part of history. No matter that straights would think of him as criminal, a blot on society. It was important to Bouchet that they should think of him in any terms. A legend didn't have to seek approval from the masses, so long as he commanded their respect.

And in his native Corsica, along the southern coast of France, throughout Algiers, Bouchet commanded that respect, to a large degree. He was the man to see—or one of several men, at any rate—for drugs or women, arms or any other contraband from Africa, America, the Middle East. He was a businessman *extraordinaire,* but he could not afford to let it rest with that. If he relaxed now, the Corsican would rot and die.

Stagnation was the enemy. The ache of promise unfulfilled. Henri had made a promise to himself that he would one day stand alone, unrivaled in his chosen field, and he would keep that promise no matter what the cost.

The Corsican shrugged away the thought of failure. There had been many setbacks along the trail that he had chosen, but he overcame them each in turn, as he would overcome the next one, and the next.

The death of the Colombian did not disturb Henri. They were competitors, at best, and the removal of competitors could only broaden opportunities for those who survived. It wasn't violence, either, that had driven him to seek the solace of the bar. The Corsican had killed a score of men himself, let contracts on at least a hundred more, and he was comfortable with violent death.

Except his own.

And that was it, of course.

The murder of the squat Colombian reminded Henri that he was not immortal. He could just as easily be gutted like a fish and left to stain the carpet of a hotel room so far from home. He could be cheated of his dream before it had a chance to ripen and drop into his waiting hands.

The tall American silently materialized beside him, a shadow perched upon the bar stool, calling softly for an ale. Henri did not acknowledge him at first, but he was checking out the man peripherally, examining the profile, the athletic build, the gun beneath his arm.

The ale arrived. The American took a sip, another, finally swivelled on his stool to face Henri.

"Too bad about Ramon."

The Corsican compelled himself to answer.

"*Oui.* Too bad."

"It sort of makes you wonder what the little bastard knew."

"I beg your pardon?"

"Hey, it fits. He tumbled onto something that he wasn't s'pose to know about, and so they iced him. Simple."

Simple, yes, except that this excursion to the Irish coast had been described as business, with a truce imposed by independent guards. With the Colombian already lying in a body bag, it looked more like war than business. Assuming that the two could ever be completely separated in the world Bouchet had chosen for himself.

"You know the guy?"

The question jarred him from his reverie.

"By reputation only," he replied.

"Same here. I guess he used to move a lot of flake."

It was incredible how easily a living man became the past tense, gone, forgotten in a day or two by everyone except his relatives and closest friends.

Henri Bouchet did not have any relatives or trusted friends. Would there by anyone to grieve for him, to hold his memory for just a day or two, when he was gone?

A lump was forming in his throat, and now he washed it down with wine. He kept a firm grip on the glass to hide the trembling of his hands.

"I figure he's the first, but not the last," the tall American confided in him, almost whispering across the foamy mug of ale.

"You think there will be more like that?"

"Why not? You get your competition all assembled in a single place, you whack 'em out an' there you are. Smooth sailing."

It was making sense, and now Bouchet had both hands on the wineglass, knuckles whitening until he thought the glass would shatter in his fist.

"Have you a suspect?"

The American was grinning at him, sharklike now. "I've got a dozen of 'em, but my money's on the guys who set the meet."

"Joe Scalish?"

"Maybe. Or the Russian he's so buddy-buddy with these days."

Bouchet had not suspected; well, perhaps a little, when he noted Soviets, the Cubans and Vietnamese. Their presence was unusual, considering the occupations and the temperament of others at the conference.

The tall American appeared to read his thoughts.

"I'm leaning toward the Russian," he decided, thinking to himself, aloud. "If he could smooth the way, his Cuban friends could corner all the snow themselves."

"It would make sense," the Corsican agreed.

"You bet your ass. An' those Vietnamese are heavy into heroin, ya know? If they could close the Turkish pipcline down..."

He didn't have to finish for Henri to understand the grim scenario.

"Have you some reason to believe that this is true?"

"I couldn't make it stick in court," the cool American replied. "It's just a feeling that I got, while I was lookin' down at poor Ramon."

"I don't believe we have been introduced."

The tall American was smiling as he reached for Henri's hand.

"The name is Black, but you can call me Mike."

FOR CHAN YUEN FAI, the death of a Colombian—or all Colombians—had no more real significance than water dumped and wasted on the sand. Mortality and death were everyday realities within the Ah Kong Triad sphere of influence, and Chan had mastered fear long ago. He knew he would die in time, but he was careful to prolong the living that preceded death. It was a duty that he owned himself, and Chan had never left a debt unpaid.

The death of the Colombian had startled some of the assembled delegates at Cashel House, but Chan, for his part, was surprised that only one had died so far. With such a crew beneath one roof, their ancient enmities allowed to simmer, thus confined, he had been waiting for a series of explosions to release the pent-up tensions. The Triad delegates had come prepared for anything, and they were ready to defend themselves if anyone should try to make a second score that afternoon.

The Japanese, of course, would be among the first to die if Chan and his companions should unleash their wrath. The tattooed men of Yakuza were merely symbols of the enduring hatred that had kept their motherlands on opposite sides of every war in living memory. From ancient times, the warlords of Nippon had treated China as their own backyard, a heathen land where they were free to rape and pillage as they pleased. These days, howevever, if they wanted any of the magic powders that the Triads could supply in such abundance, there would be a heavy price to pay.

Another problem, equally abrasive, was the presence of Vietnamese in the assemblage. To Chan they were godless animals, and he despised them for their politics, their atheism, their alliance with the rebel bastards who controlled his native land. While he and his associates were forced to live in Burma, Thailand or the crowded Hong Kong colony, Vietnamese and other half-breed scum were being showered with the wealth of China by the Peking government, instructed in the art of spreading revolution through the East.

It would have pleased him to destroy them all—Vietnamese and Japanese alike—but Chan was first of all a businessman, and he would not reject a profit made at the expense of his ancestral enemies. In fact, it would be sweet to line his pockets with their cash. The killing would come later, when he had the strength to take them all at once.

Until that time, he would enjoy the fine cuisine at Cashel House and listen, learn, prepare himself for what was meant to be. Conglomeration was the future, clearly, and the Triads could not easily afford to be left out. If they should try to go it on their own, the mere supply of heroin alone would not allow them to succeed. There were the Turks, the Mexicans and untold others, waiting with their stockpiles of inferior supplies, all hungry for the markets that the Triads presently controlled. Chan Fai could not afford to throw it all away.

Later, the time would be ripe.

He smiled and sipped the Irish coffee, savoring its rich aroma. He enjoyed the luxuries that came with money, power and prestige. Before the conference was finished, Chan would have a great deal more of each. He would be going home victorious, a secret hero to the Triad legions who were waiting for his every word.

A moving shadow in the corner of his eye alerted Chan to the approach of an intruder on his private space. He glanced up quickly, recognized the tall American from dinner and the meetings of the early afternoon. He was the man called Black, and there were rumors that his presence at the conference was a source of irritation to Joe Scalish and some others in the stateside Mafia. A man to watch.

"You're Chan?"

The Triad leader nodded.

"Michael Black."

"I recognize you, Mr. Black."

"We need to talk."

Chan gestured vaguely toward an empty chair across the table from himself, and the American sat down.

"I never like to beat around the bush," he said. "How close are you to Joey Scalish and the New York crowd?"

"We share a common interest," Chan replied.

"Would it surprise you if I said he's looking for another source?"

Chan kept his face impassive, broken by an enigmatic smile. "A businessman is always looking, I believe."

"Another source for your supply?"

Chan felt the smile begin to slip, and caught it just before it got away. He waited, saying nothing, while the American observed him from behind his mirrored glasses, watching, waiting. When the silence had stretched out between them for a moment, more, the man called Black leaned forward, speaking in a confidential tone.

"You've noticed Scalish getting chummy with the Russian and his buddies from Hanoi?"

Chan nodded. He had noticed everything.

"The word I get, they're thinking maybe the Vietnamese could run your action better than it's being run right now."

A cool smile spread across Chan's face.

"I wonder why you tell me this?"

"Hey, that's no mystery. I hate that fucking Scalish. He's a weasel, an' he'd stab his mother in the back if he could make a dime."

"Why come to me?"

"Because some other people think you run your end just right. They won't be happy dealing with Manhattan or those zipper-heads from Nam."

"A business interest, then."

"Hell, yes. But that still leaves some room for personal concerns. I guess you'd say I naturally lean toward anybody Scalish tries to screw."

"Assuming that your information should prove accurate—"

"It's accurate, all right."

"Assuming it is, I question whether the Vietnamese could operate successfully in my domain."

"Tha's why they're bringing in the Japs."

Chan stiffened, caught himself and instantly displayed composure to his guest.

"Go on."

"The way I hear it, Scalish and the man from Moscow have been talking to the Yakuza for weeks. We're even getting rumbles out in Vegas about the change that's in the wind."

"I see."

It made a twisted kind of sense to Chan. If Scalish and the Communists desired his territory, it would be wise to field a foreign army, using mercenaries to reduce their losses and divert suspicion from themselves. A Yakuza invasion of the fat narcotics trade would not be any great surprise, and it would leave the money men, the masterminds, secure behind their foreign barricades.

Except that Chan could see them now, and recognize them each for what they were—provided the American was not distorting facts for reasons of his own.

"I will consider what you say."

"That's all I ask. An' watch yourself, okay?"

"I always do."

Chan Fai would watch himself a good deal closer, with the American's pronouncement fresh in mind. He would be watching Michael Black, as well, and seeking concrete reasons why the man would come to him, alert him to the danger—if there was a danger—when he might as easily have let it go. He was an errand boy, that much was clear, and Chan was sure that therein lay the source of his concern.

Above all else, Chan would be watching Scalish, the Vietnamese, the Yakuza. He had already recognized the danger they posed, but it was closer now and more immediate. The Triad chief could not afford to let them take him by surprise.

If Michael Black was accurate in his surmise, the hostile move would not occur at Cashel House. The conference would be used to pacify the troops, to lay out territories on a map, distribute the imaginary slices of a global pie. It would be later, when the Triad delegates had reached their homes, that Yakuza assassins would make their move.

Assuming that he let them have the time.

If Michael Black was accurate, then Chan would have to strike before the others had a chance. Perhaps tonight, tomorrow; soon. If he allowed them to disperse, to pass on their orders, he would be soon confronted with an army clamoring against his gates, demanding blood.

His blood.

There were ways of striking, even here, that would not bear his mark. So far the Yakuza and the Vietnamese, the Soviets and Scalish, were attempting to unite on common ground. If Chan could destroy that bond, the threat against his Triads would evaporate.

The smile was back, inscrutable as ever, and he sipped the Irish coffee, staring through its steam to an imaginary point a thousand miles away. He did not hear the waitress or the delegates around him, clinking glasses, laughing softly, mulling over business in their several dialects. His mind was far away, following the convoluted corridors of treachery. There was an enemy to be defeated, and he meant to do it before his time ran short.

It was another debt that Chan did not intend to leave unpaid.

17

With his index finger, Seamus Kelly traced the outline of a bullet hole in the Saab. Then he finally straightened up, a frown etched deep into his face. The rented car had taken quite a pounding; the driver, Michael Black, was lucky just to be alive.

Or was he, now?

The Russian, Gladnikov, might have some plans for Black, and for the lady, too, when he digested everything that Kelly had unloaded on him in the dining room. He might begin to think in terms of treachery, and Kelly knew from past experience that people who betrayed the Russian wound up dead. Or worse.

It might be worse for Bridget Chambers if Gladnikov marked her for a traitor.

He walked around the Saab again, scowling as he examined the damage. The driver had to be a pro at killing—at avoiding being killed—to turn this kind of ambush into victory. He should have been stretched out in County Galway's modest morgue by now, but there were five or six men lying in his place.

It was obvious to Kelly that Michael Black was nothing like the others at the conference. They were essentially a ruthless breed of businessmen, long years removed from the reality of violence in the streets. They gave the orders now, dispatched the troops, but Kelly doubted whether any of them had fired a shot in anger since they learned to ride in limousines with bodyguards to watch their backs.

This Michael Black was something else, a soldier, the kind of man who handled his problems by himself, and in a way that guaranteed they did not recur. He had already killed five men today, and Kelly had no doubt that he would kill a dozen more, two dozen if it came to that. He was a breed apart, and the IRA commander wondered what his mission was at Cashel House.

He was aware of all the rumors current at the conference, including rumbles of a rift within the stateside Mafia. The Western families had pooled their strength behind a single representative, according to the line, and they had chosen Michael Black to speak for them at Cashel House. It fit, all right, but there was more behind the scenes, and Kelly was determined to know everything.

The syndicate did not intrigue him even slightly, but his role as the security consultant for the conference made it essential for him to know each mobster for precisely who and what he was, in order to protect them from each other and from the outside world. He had fumbled with the Colombian; Kelly would not face embarrassment a second time. He could not easily afford to have the Russian think him weak or inefficient. Others in the IRA would be glad to take his place if he could not command respect from their suppliers, keep the lines for arms and ammunition open, flowing smoothly to the war zones in the north.

He had to determine who was hunting Michael Black, and why they had elected to come gunning for him in County Galway. If it was a private feud, he could defuse it for the moment, let it be settled on other turf, another time. But if it sprang out of the conference itself, that was a more difficult matter.

The IRA commander snapped his fingers, and a silent figure suddenly emerged from concealment in the trees. The rifleman was dressed in forest camouflage, his face and hands obscured by battlefield cosmetics, and he held his automatic rifle like the pure professional he was. He took up station near the Saab and waited for his orders.

"Put a watch on this around the clock. It doesn't leave without my personal permission."

"Yessir."

"I'll be needing a shadow on the guest in number 42, as well. He had a lucky break today, but we'll not be wanting the fireworks slopping over here."

"It's as good as done."

His orders would be relayed around the grounds and obeyed. His soldiers knew the penalty for failure. The rifleman before him and others stationed on the grounds would rather be at home in Ulster, carrying their war against the common enemy. The IRA commander felt that way himself. But he could not risk offending Gladnikov, their only ally with a boundless cache of arms at his disposal.

He put the home front out of mind, and concentrated on the task at hand. He would be called upon to answer for the whereabouts of Michael Black at any given time, and to protect him from attack unless Alexei passed along a different word. In that event, he might be called upon to kill the soldier from America, and Kelly wasn't looking forward to that at all.

The man was nothing to him, personally, but he had already seen what Michael Black could do. He would be vulnerable here, cut off inside the grounds, without his wheels, but still . . .

There would be hell to pay if it came to that, and Seamus Kelly hoped that Gladnikov and the rest could find a way to settle up their debts outside when everything was done at Cashel House. He wanted them gone.

God *damn* the Russian for electing to convene his meeting here.

God *damn* the grim American for bringing in his private war.

God damn them all.

They just might be the death of Seamus Kelly yet.

BRIDGET CHAMBERS STEPPED OUT of the shower and reached for a towel from the rack, snugging it around her body. For a moment, she studied her eyes, her face, in the full-length bathroom mirror for any telltale sign of guilt that might betray her to Alexei Gladnikov.

No sign.

She smiled, relaxing slightly, beginning to dry herself with the towel. It might be ego, but she felt that she could deal with Gladnikov. He would forgive an infidelity, assuming he found out. There might be trouble for a while, perhaps a macho show of anger with a slap or two, but nothing she could not defuse in time. The lady knew her talents and abilities on both sides of the sheets, and the Russian had grown used to her. He trusted her as much as he was capable of trusting anyone. He would believe her story if she sold it earnestly, with true conviction. He would let her have a second chance.

Unless, of course, he had some reason to suspect her of a greater treachery than casual sex. In that case . . .

Bridget put the prospect out of mind and concentrated on the tall American, the man who had somehow, impossibly, discovered her identity, her link with Interpol. He did not mean to sell her out, she knew that much, but there was something different about him, in his attitude, the way he made his presence felt.

And she had felt his presence, right enough. The memory of *that* was strong enough to make her blush, and Bridget took a moment to compose herself. There was no time for girlish crushes now, no place for an infatuation that could easily prove disastrous. Their moment had been brief and powerful—but it was done, a piece of history, unlikely to repeat itself.

Bridget Chambers knew the risks of letting her emotions get involved on a job as critical as this. At best it made an agent careless and resulted in performance that was less than satisfactory. At worst, it got an agent killed, and sometimes very messily, too.

She finished drying off and hung the towel back in its place, reaching for her bathrobe as she heard Alexei enter, close the door behind him and double-check the lock. He called her softly from the foyer of the suite.

"In here."

She belted up the robe, allowing it to flare in front so as to show off her cleavage, and was almost to the door when it swung inward. Alexei stood there watching her, his Slavic face expressionless. He glanced from Bridget to the shower, back again, before he spoke.

"You are not feeling well?"

"I'm fine."

His tone was distant. Somewhere inside Bridget's head a small alarm was going off.

"A shower in the afternoon?"

"It felt refreshing. I was tired."

"I have not seen you shower in the middle of the day, except when we have been together, ah?"

The smile felt frozen on her face.

"But you have not been here."

"Of course."

"Alexei, are you jealous? Is there something I have done?"

"Perhaps I should be asking you."

She felt as if her face might crack wide open, but she kept the frozen smile in place.

"Alexei, come."

She took him by the hand and led him toward the bed. An unobtrusive movement freed the belt around her waist, allowed the folds of Bridget's silken robe to separate, revealing her from throat to floor. She drew herself against him, pressed her lips against the hollow of his throat.

"You need me now," she whispered heatedly. "This business of the meetings makes you tense."

"Perhaps."

His hand was on her naked breast, moving downward now, seeking out the center of her warmth. His fingers found a rhythm of their own, and Bridget melted into him.

The sudden pain was blinding, unimaginable, robbing her of any power to fight or scream. She felt her legs begin to fold, and she was falling, tumbling backward, on her way before his fist exploded in her face.

It was incredible, this pain. She couldn't move. Her lower body felt like broken glass, and now the right side of her face was swelling, going numb, and she could taste the blood inside her mouth.

He knows.

The certainty was worse than any pain, because it spoke of agony to come, and Bridget fought to get her strength back now, to roll away and run, escape at any cost. It didn't matter that she would be running naked, out of danger into danger. Anything was better than Alexei, now that he knew.

Knew what?

That she had gone to bed with Michael Black?

That she was Interpol?

No time to puzzle out the answers, She was doomed if she remained inside the suite.

A twisting, rolling motion, and her lower body screamed in protest, flashing angry signals to her brain. The sheets and blanket seemed like quicksand, sucking at her, holding her in place, and Bridget knew that it was hopeless, even as Alexei struck again.

She saw the fist this time, and attempted to evade the crushing blow, but succeeded only in deflecting it a fraction. He was aiming for her nose, her lips, but Bridget twisted, took it on her cheek, and felt the fragile bone give way with a disgusting snap. The impact stretched her out across the mattress, on her back.

From somewhere miles above, she heard Alexei's voice.

"We have so much to talk about," he said. "I wouldn't think of letting you go out before we have our little chat. And afterward—"

It took a moment for her ringing ears to recognize the wheezing sound as laughter filtered through the echo chamber of her pain. He was enjoying this too much to let it end, no matter what she told him now, no matter what she did.

The certainty of death was like a vacuum chamber in her chest, beneath her heart, a hollowness that made her want to scream and weep and vomit, all at once. If he continued, she knew there was no hope. No hope at all.

And in the certainty of death she found a new resolve to see it through and make him show his worst, see how much she could endure before she broke. If she could make him kill her before she told him anything, it would be something. Not a victory, of course, but something less than a defeat.

She felt him leaning close to her, smelled the whiskey on his foul breath. He gripped her face in viselike fingers, shook her head, demanding that she look at him while he decreed her fate.

Gathering all her courage and strength, she spit directly in his face, her bloody spittle clinging to his forehead, dribbling in crimson rivulets across his cheeks. He stared at her, enraged.

"What now?" she asked, hoping he could understand her through her swollen, bleeding lips. "Will you be man enough to take me now?"

Alexei smiled, his face a grisly death mask hovering above her own. And when he came for her, there wasn't even time to raise her hands.

18

"I'm tellin' ya, we're gonna get the short end of the stick from all'a this."

Esquilante forked another chunk of steak into his mouth, began to chew it, but he never missed a beat.

"That friggin' Scalish means to have the whole pot for himself, you mark my words."

"Damn straight."

The echo came from Kansas City's delegate, Ernie Barboza, who sat beside the corpulent Chicago mobster, barely picking at his food.

Mack Bolan glanced at the dais, back again at Esquilante, feigning interest in the mafioso's words.

"You got a plan to turn this thing around?"

Chicago grinned around his steak. "I might. I might, at that."

"I'm listening."

"Well, not so fast. We gotta know exac'ly who our friends are, right? I mean, it wouldn't do for me to jus' go on about a thing like that, an' find out later you was on the other side."

The soldier shrugged. "I told you once, I work for anyone who pays the tab. Right now, my backers aren't exactly setting up a Scalish fan club, if you get my drift."

"Things change."

"*Some* things."

"You gonna give the guy a bad report?"

Esquilante's rodent eyes gleamed. He had the scent of blood now, and he couldn't let it go.

"I'm going to report exactly what I've seen and heard."

"Which is?"

He hesitated, letting Esquilante think he was concerned about the import of his words. In fact, his eyes were on the Russian's table now, where Gladnikov's usual party seemed to be one member short.

"I think there's too much Scalish in the deal," he said at last. "Too much New York. I think, for damn sure, that there's too much red around to suit my taste."

"All right."

Chicago's spokesman rocked back in his chair and glanced at Kansas City with a twinkle in his eye. Barboza shrugged in answer, bobbed his head in what Bolan took for casual consent.

"We think alike," Chicago told him, leaning forward conspiratorially, stoking in a forkful of potatoes. "I think we can do business here."

"Still listening."

But Bolan's mind was on Gladnikov and on Bridget Chambers. She had not come down for dinner. He felt a nameless dread well up inside himself, nibbling around the edges of his stomach, sending icy tendrils up his spine.

She should have been there, and Bolan started going through the mental list of reasons for her absence, listening to Esquilante with a portion of his mind and nodding when appropriate, replying to the mobster with a string of monosyllables that told him they were still in tune.

She might be feeling ill, of course, but why?

The food? Improbable in the extreme.

She might be resting, begging off dinner, but it struck him that Gladnikov would not accept excuses from the members of his retinue. They would be at his side, or he would know the reason why.

She might have faked an illness, to give herself some stretch, a chance to search Alexei's things, or even work on other rooms, as she had gone through Bolan's the night before. It was a risky proposition, but Bridget Chambers had the nerve.

At worst, of course, the Russian might have found her out somehow. He might have harmed her in his anger, in his haste to learn the secrets that she knew. It had been hours since they met in Bolan's room. That was time enough.

Revolted by the images that came unbidden to his mind, the Executioner had lost his appetite, but he continued eating, forcing down the excellent meal, feigning attentiveness to Esquilante and his plans.

The guy was talking revolution, and Bolan didn't plan to interrupt while he was on a roll. If Esquilante and Barboza stayed on track, Joe Scalish and his people could expect some trouble from the hinterlands.

The party was beginning to disintegrate as diners here and there declined dessert, excused themselves for yet another round of meetings that would last late into the night. They had so little time now, less than a full working day to cinch the deals that they had flown around the world to make. If they were going to secure their places in the new regime, they had to do it now, tonight.

Except that Bolan had some other plans in mind for each and every one of the assembled delegates. The men around him had grown soft, from all appearances, forgetting where they came from, all the lessons of the streets and slums that made them what they were today. And it was time for a refresher course to put their world back in perspective, let them know that they were not the kings they thought themselves to be.

It would be Bolan's certain pleasure to instruct them in the art of staying humble, scrambling for their lives, and anyone who failed the course was *out,* once and for all. Survivors would be free to take the message home and spread it through the ranks—in Bangkok, Bogotá, Marseilles, wherever. Bolan was preparing to instruct them on a global scale.

But first, the woman.

Before he made his move he had to know if she was working, injured or—

"An' tha's exac'ly what I'll tell 'em," Esquilante rasped, another heaping forkload damming up his monologue at last. "You wif me?"

Bolan smiled and laid his fork aside, pushed back his plate.

"Let's say I haven't heard a thing I disagreed with yet."

Chicago's eyes were beaming at him, as the capo smiled.

"So, we gotta deal?"

"I'll have to talk it over with my sponsors."

"I know all that, an' they'll be acting on whatever you run down. So, have we got a deal?"

"I'd say we've got a deal."

They shook, Barboza getting in on it as something of an afterthought, and Bolan rose to leave.

"I've got some people left to see," he said. "We wouldn't want to make them think it's in the bag."

The wisdom of it tickled Esquilante, and he grinned, exposing teeth congested with a residue of steak and salad.

"Sure. Go on, enjoy yourself. We'll talk again when we get home."

"All right."

When we get home.

Except that some of them were never going home again, at least alive. Mack Bolan might be one of those who could lose it here, but if he did, the soldier would not go alone. He had a job to do, and he would see it finished to the best of his ability, or die in the attempt.

But right now, there was Bridget Chambers.

"SO, WHAT'S THE BEEF?"

Joe Scalish settled down into his padded chair across from Gladnikov and watched the Russian closely, searching for a clue that would explain his sudden sense of urgency.

"We have a problem, a potential problem."

"Oh, yeah? What's that?"

He tried to keep it breezy, but the short hairs on the mafioso's neck were standing at attention now. He knew damn well the Russian wouldn't sit him down to talk about a problem with the plumbing or the kitchen help.

"There may be someone here who works against us," Gladnikov replied.

Joe Scalish felt himself relax. Almost.

"That's it? We knew from the beginning that we couldn't get them all. So what? We give 'em time to think it over, an' if anybody still won't come around, we cut 'em off. They can't do business long without supplies."

The Russian shook his head, scowling, a teacher trying to explain a problem to a stubborn or retarded child.

"I am not speaking of your competition, Joseph. We will deal with them as we agreed."

The prickling of his scalp was back, in spades. "Then who?"

"A traitor."

"Huh? What kind of... Hey, you mean a fed?"

"Perhaps. Or Interpol, the Sûreté, the drug enforcement people. Any one of them, or perhaps all of them."

Joe Scalish shook his head.

"Tha's crazy, man. We've got security, you understand? I know these guys. I won't pretend we always get along, but shit, they sure as hell aren't cops."

"You know them all?"

The little smile informed Joe Scalish that Alexei recognized his lie for what it was.

"Well, some of them I know only by reputation, sure, but I checked them out. You checked them out."

"Agreed. Which does not prove that we were not deceived."

"Well, shit, with our security—"

"We have already lost one delegate, with an attempt on another."

"I explained all that. I'm working on it. Anyhow, the feds don't come in killing people. Not where I'm from, anyway."

Another Slavic scowl. "What do you know about the man in number 42, this Michael Black?"

And it was Joey's turn to frown. "The guy's a wild card, if you get my drift. He plays the field. You got the price, he's yours. A hitter. One of maybe half a dozen who can tag their target anytime and anywhere. He sure as hell ain't working for the government."

"You know him, then. By sight?"

"Well, no. I told you, he's a wild card. Like the Aces in the old days, eh? They change their faces and their names like most guys change their socks."

"So you have never met this Michael Black before?"

"Not face to face. He did some work for Augie in the old days, when the Talifero boys were still around and goin' strong. These days, I understand he's more or less a free-lance, mostly working in the West."

"I understand that there have been some problems with your Western families."

"They're not *my* families, okay? You gotta understan', we got this council, eh? Right now, I've got the weight on my side, but the boys out west, a few down south, could be they want a bigger piece of pie. So what? You think they're gonna blow it all by workin' with the feds? That's nuts."

The Russian shrugged.

"I only know what I have seen. A member of my own concern has been in touch with Michael Black, possibly discussing certain things that are very confidential. There may be cause for some concern."

"Your people? Jesus, do you mean to say *you've* got a leak?"

"The problem was corrected earlier this afternoon. It will not recur. I wanted to discuss the matter privately with you before we make a move against this 'wild card,' as you call him.''

Scalish felt another little chill along his spine, and there was gooseflesh rising on his arms.

"Slow down a minute, willya? We can't just start blasting here. We got a sit-down going on, for Chrissake. It'll ruin everything."

Alexei shook his head, released a weary sigh.

"I never intimated that the action should be public, Joseph, or that it should necessarily be taken here, tonight. We still have time to put our house in order, but we must be very careful now, and not throw anything away."

"I understand. We've had a microscope on Black since someone tried to shoot him up this morning. Anything he tries, he's in the bag."

"All right. If you are confident that we control the situation . . ."

"Piece of cake. No sweat."

The frown was back in place, but now the Russian kept his peace and merely nodded, letting Scalish know that it was in his hands.

And on his head, if anything went wrong.

It was his job to see that nothing did go wrong. And if the wild card tried to deal one off the bottom of the deck tonight or tomorrow, he was in for a surprise. There were a lot of ways to deal with problems of that sort, and Joey Scalish knew them all.

Whichever way it went, he would be coming out on top. He was a born survivor, and there was no way he would let the Russian take him for a ride. The conference was his, no matter what they thought in Moscow, and he might be forced to issue some reminders somewhere down the road.

Joe Scalish was on top, and he was staying there. The rest of them were second best, and seconds didn't count at all.

MACK BOLAN DOUBLE-CHECKED the Beretta's load and jacked a live one into the firing chamber, testing the familiar feel of the weapon in his hand before returning it to leather. The weight of it was comforting beneath his arm.

He was in blacksuit, face and hands discolored with combat cosmetics, ready for the night. Unless he picked more up along the way, the 93-R, with a slim stiletto and garrote, would be his only weapons for the strike. He had been forced to travel light in County Galway, but with any luck at all, the armament on hand would do.

His suite was all in darkness, and he faced the open window now, his eyes adjusting to the night outside. The sun set late in western Ireland, but finally the gardens were cloaked in shadow, tempered by the promise of a rising moon. He had to make his move before the moon arrived, or the filtered light would make him visible. He had to be about his business now, before the night got any older, and before his quarry had a chance to break their meetings, separate, return to their rooms.

The IRA commandos might be watching, Bolan knew, but there was nothing he could do about it now. He could not risk approaching Gladnikov's preserve directly, through the corridors. There would be too much risk of an open confrontation before he was ready to bring the curtain down. He had to get inside, find out if Bridget Chambers was alive, before he let the fire storm loose at Cashel House.

Another moment, searching, feeling out the night with ears and eyes. If they were watching him, he couldn't spot them in the trees. A sniper might be set to pick him off as soon as he cleared the windowsill, and then again they might be satisfied to track him, catch him in the act and corner him inside the Russian's suite. In either case, he would be dead.

Still, he had no choice. He had to satisfy himself about the lady.

And if his fears were realized, then he would have a final meeting with Gladnikov.

The soldier wriggled through the open window, setting down without a sound amid the shrubbery outside. He hit a combat crouch and waited for the bullet to explode between his eyes, the warning shout to bring his enemies. Only silence kept him company in the night. In another moment, caution winning over haste, the Executioner began to move.

The Russian's suite was at the rear of the hotel, and Bolan circled the building, clinging to the shadows. He sprinted low and fast across the open spaces where the undergrowth was trimmed away. If there were sentries watching him they kept their distance in the darkness, letting Bolan make his run unopposed.

He recognized the Russian's suite at once, with curtains open, lights ablaze. He huddled in the darkness, scanning, recognizing that the suite was deserted.

The bathroom door was open, offering a wedge of darkness that enticed the eye, invited him inside. It might be nothing, and again, it might hold everything he had come to learn.

Another glance around, and Bolan moved. He would be framed against the light, but there was nothing he could do about that now. He had to play the cards as they were dealt, and never mind the risk. A window had been left ajar, and Bolan worked it open with his fingers, aware of what a perfect target he presented in silhouette. His shoulders prickled where the bullet would come burning in if anyone should spot him now. A roving sentry or deliberate tail could take him and he would never even hear the fatal shot.

He slipped inside and drew the curtains shut. If he had not been spotted as he entered, he was clear from that direction now. But he was running out of time.

He crossed the suite and threw the bathroom door wide open. His hand slid along the wall to the light switch, threw it, brought the room alive.

Almost.

He found her in the tub.

Gladnikov had wrapped her body in a pair of giant towels. They had absorbed the blood, or most of it at any rate, in brilliant tie-dyed patterns corresponding to her wounds. The soldier knew that she was dead, his mind screamed out that he had come too late, and still he forced himself to peel the bloody towels away.

There was a ringing in his ears, and Bolan felt the old, familiar tightness in his throat, as if a fist was clenched around his Adam's apple, threatening to strangle him. He swallowed hard and rubbed a forearm roughly back and forth across his burning eyes. The remnants of his dinner did a lazy barrel roll and settled restlessly beneath his ribs.

Goddamn it!

Bolan carefully replaced the towels, as if afraid to hurt or disturb her. Her blood was on his fingers now.

Her blood was on his soul.

He rose and turned away, his fingers leaving bloody tracks across the plaster as he killed the lights. She would rest easier in darkness, and there would be time for revelations later, when his job was done.

The soldier still had work to do.

And as he cleared the bathroom doorway, Bolan knew at once that he was not alone. A fleeting image in the corner of his eye, and he was turning into confrontation with the threat before it registered in conscious thought.

The IRA commando stood perhaps ten feet away, between Mack Bolan and the bed, his M-16 held level at his waist. His hands were steady, but there was a nervousness about the eyes, as if he wasn't sure precisely what should happen next.

The hellfire warrior didn't give him time to think about it. Feinting to the right, he was already ducking, weaving, as the automatic rifle stuttered into life. A line of tumblers sliced the air above his head, their racket filling up the suite, but Bolan was already closing for the kill. He threw a solid shoulder block into the gunner's ribs, imploding startled lungs, and sent the rifle spinning from his grasp. A follow-through, and they were thrashing on the bed together, gouging, clawing, each one seeking the advantage that would bring him through alive.

An elbow to the windpipe ended all the gunner's opposition, left him shuddering and gagging out his life as Bolan rolled away. He watched the dying soldier for a moment, finally leaned across with the stiletto in his hand and finished it, the sharp steel making another opening beneath his chin.

Bolan stooped, unbuckled the dead man's cartridge belt and adjusted it to fit his waist. He scooped up the fallen rifle and checked its action, finding it undamaged from the drop. He was already in the window, sliding clear before the other delegates could possibly identify the rifle fire or trace it to the source.

One down and plenty left to go.

Assuming that he had the time, the chance to take them out.

Unless they killed him first.

But one of them, at any rate, would have to go. The Russian, Gladnikov. His fate was sealed if Bolan had to walk through fire, unarmed, to rip his throat out empty-handed.

For Bridget.

For all the blood on Bolan's soul.

For all the unpaid debts he owed Gladnikov and his kind.

The Executioner was rolling out in frenzy mode, and God help anyone who tried to stop him now.

19

"Goddammit, I know gunfire when I hear it," Scalish snapped, infuriated by the fact that Seamus Kelly did not cringe from his display of rage. "I'm telling you it came from somewhere on this wing."

"We're checking on it," Kelly told him evenly, refusing to be cowed. His eyes were level and unflinching.

The two of them were faced off in the eastern wing of the hotel, surrounded by a squad of Kelly's IRA commandos dressed in camouflage and brandishing M-16s. The odds would normally have made him feel uneasy, but the capo from New York was riding on his fury now, and it had given him the momentary courage to defy the guns.

"Check faster, dammit," he demanded, feeling color in his face. "I can't afford another fuck-up like the one with the Colombian."

Before the IRA commander could respond a couple of his soldiers cleared the corner of the hallway, Ian Duffy wedged between them, looking frightened as he had every right to be. Joe Scalish brushed past his captain of security to meet the pale proprietor of Cashel House.

"You got a passkey on you?"

Duffy nodded weakly. "Yessir."

"Well, we've got ourselves a little problem here. There were some shots somewhere in this wing, but it's a little hard to pin them down. We need to check the rooms."

The hotel man fished in his pocket and brought out the key ring, offering it to Scalish in a trembling hand. The

New York mafioso stepped aside and turned his gaze on Kelly once again.

"You take it," he commanded. "This is your department."

Kelly glowered at the keys, as if the act of touching them would make him personally responsible for anything they found inside the rooms. A heartbeat passed before he took the ring from Duffy, passed it to the closest rifleman and jerked his head in the direction of the corridor behind him.

"Go."

The gunners fanned out swiftly, expertly. Joe Scalish thought about their war up north, the house-to-house fighting, and realized that in all probability they had been through this sort of thing before. These men were rough, all right, surpassing anything he had back home for discipline and grim efficiency. He wondered idly what it would cost to take a couple dozen of them home.

They were already checking out the closest of the empty rooms, one man up front to lead the way, the others close behind him, crouched behind their weapons like the members of a SWAT team closing for the kill. A moment, and they were emerging, crossing to the suite directly opposite, their silent faces telling Scalish they had come up empty.

And again.

They were emerging from the fourth suite and moving on the fifth when Scalish heard a group of delegates approaching from the direction of the dining room. He couldn't understand their words, but from the tone he knew that they were angry, frightened, anxious to be out of there and moving on to any place beyond the line of fire. He felt his dream begin to buckle, cracking at the seams, and bitterness welled up inside him, tasting sour in his mouth.

"We don't need that," he said, as half a dozen angry men came into view around the corner of the hallway, hesitating at the sight of all those guns.

The IRA commander took his cue and sent a team of riflemen to head them off and hold them where they were, preventing them from interfering with the search. The other guns were on the fifth suite down already, crowding through the door, their rifles at the ready.

One of them emerged, eyes dark and angry as he flashed the thumbs-up signal to his chief. Joe Scalish followed Kelly down the corridor and through the doorway of the suite he recognized as Gladnikov's.

Inside, they found an IRA commando stretched across the bed, his nose smashed flat across his face, his throat an open wound from ear to ear. The blood from that horrendous gash had soaked through bedspread, blanket, sheet and all, leaving only a bluish corpse behind. In a glance, Joe Scalish saw that the gunner's rifle and his ammunition belt were gone.

Goddammit.

There was a trace of gunsmoke in the air, and a ragged line of holes across the ceiling just above the door. Scalish recognized it as reflexive fire, perhaps a burst cut loose before the soldier died. He hadn't scored with any of his rounds, that much was certain, and their killer now possessed an M-16 with ammunition, to supplement his knife.

An IRA commando was already staking out the open window, staring into darkness at the gardens. Scalish had the feeling they were being watched, perhaps by someone who would have killed them all, if given half a chance.

"Let's shut those curtains, huh? Our boy's got hardware now. No point in setting up a shooting gallery."

It took a nod from Seamus Kelly to complete the chain and get his order carried out, but Scalish let it pass. There would be enough time for settling their differences when all of this was finished. He was wondering how one of Kelly's troopers came to be inside the Russian's suite, when they were hailed from the direction of the bathroom.

"Here. Come have a look at this lot, then."

Joe Scalish got there first and crowded past the soldier who had called them, glancing briefly at the sink, already startled by a mirror image of the blood before he turned toward the tub. When he recognized the woman, he felt his stomach turn over as he crossed the room to stand by the shower stall.

He hadn't seen a mess like that in years, not since the Talifero boys were still around and their gestapo used to practice seeing how damn long they could protract a dying pigeon's mortal agony. This couldn't hold a candle to the Talifero boys, but it was bad enough. Someone had worked the lady over like they meant it, and Scalish felt a cold chill creeping up his spine. He reached out blindly, found the frosted sliding door and drew it closed to hide the raw atrocity inside.

He wondered if Gladnikov would be startled, sickened by the sight, or if he might have done the job himself. It posed some ugly questions, but if the Russian *had* killed the woman, he most emphatically had *not* dispatched the soldier in the other room. That made three dead so far, with two or even three cold-blooded killers wandering the grounds of Cashel House.

Joe Scalish almost laughed aloud, remembering that almost everybody on the grounds were killers with investments to protect and scores to settle. There were too many suspects for him to play Sherlock Holmes and select the guilty party.

The New York mafioso wished that he could put the place behind him, fly back to Manhattan and to safety. It would be so easy, except that everything that happened here until the meeting adjourned was his responsibility. The conference was his idea, his dream, and he was on the hook whether it seemed fair or not.

So he had a killer to root out before the whole damned house of cards collapsed around his head. Scalish knew that if it fell apart, he would be held responsible by all concerned, and that was something that could give a capo nightmares. Back home, he had an army at his beck and call, but he was not prepared to fight the whole damned world. No way.

He was running out of time, wasting precious moments standing here, staring at the scarlet splashes on the bathroom tile.

He still had work to do, and underneath the sudden, unaccustomed fear, Scalish was looking forward to meeting the man who had disrupted his dream. He didn't give a damn, right now, precisely who he was. He had a score to settle, for himself and for the others who had put their trust in his assurances that they would be protected here.

Before the night was over, Scalish meant to settle all his debts.

MACK BOLAN WORE THE SHADOWS of the garden like a cloak, his painted hands and face, his blacksuit merging with the night and making him nearly invisible. He knew that he was not alone, but the commotion in the house had drawn a number of the sentries off, allowing him more freedom as he planned his next assault.

There was no question of retreating now, of posing as a delegate surprised and frightened by the violence gripping Cashel House. The time had come to bring the curtain down.

He wanted Gladnikov so badly he could taste it, but other delegates demanded his attention first. He could not afford to let them go unscathed. He had already played upon their fears and bigotry, and now he had to drive the lesson home. He needed chaos to complete and complement the strike, to demonstrate emphatically that there were no safe havens in the world.

Sure he was alone, Bolan moved, a gliding midnight shadow on the garden path. As he circled past the entrance to the parking lot, emerging from the undergrowth and onto open ground, he kept the grand hotel always in sight. Hesitating, knowing there was no damned way to second-guess the odds, he broke from cover, sprinting across the lawn and flower beds and driveway, less than thirty yards from the hotel, and slid into cover on the other side.

He waited breathlessly for the alarms, the shots that would reveal him and bring the troopers rushing down on him from every side. But only silence greeted him this time, and finally he started moving once again, positioning himself so that he had a field of fire in the direction of the lighted dining room.

From where he crouched in darkness, Bolan could see half a dozen delegates still seated, engrossed in conversation and apparently oblivious to the disturbance in the eastern wing of the hotel. He recognized Chan, the Triad leader, and some of his associates, their faces somber as they huddled over Irish coffee, arguing some point beyond the windowpane.

Bolan knelt as he brought the rifle to his shoulder, lining up the sights. The tumbling projectiles of the M-16 would be a bit erratic after smashing through the windowpane, and Bolan made a slight adjustment, wishing to avoid a massacre so early in the game. He wanted Chan alive and kicking, with a large enough contingent of his men to form a fighting nucleus. A couple of the flankers, though, might be expendable.

He stroked the trigger of his captured M-16 and held the weapon steady as it shuddered in his hands, dispatching 5.56 mm death and 750 rounds per minute in a single, searing burst. The brilliant muzzle-flash left tiny luminescent sparks dancing before his eyes.

Downrange, the dining room windows erupted in a spray of fractured glass, and the nearest of the Triad delegates went down, punched sideways by a spiral burst that threw him completely from his chair. Before his twitching corpse touched down, a second target detonated into flying blood and tissue, toppling with sufficient energy to kick over the table, spilling Irish coffee and food as the survivors scattered for their lives. ·

They fell to the floor at once, and Bolan let them go, his secondary burst a warning rather than a serious attempt to root them out. He stitched a ragged figure eight across the upturned tabletop, then withdrew, knowing that the sentries would be coming.

They couldn't miss him, his display of fireworks, and if none of them had visually marked his last position, it wouldn't taken them long to pin it down. He meant to give himself some combat stretch before that happened, and meet the IRA commandos on his own terms. If nothing else, at least he could assure himself a fighting chance.

In the dining room, his frightened targets would be brushing off the shattered glass and wasted food, and heading cautiously toward the exits. They would be intent on clearing out, on putting Cashel House behind them, and short of violence there would be no way for Scalish to prolong their stay. The summit conference was over, and the would-be king was as good as dead.

It was a job that he was looking forward to. First Scalish, then the Russian, Gladnikov. He owed them both a heavy payback, and their tab was coming due right here, right now.

The Executioner was one with darkness as he sought his prey. The night enveloped him and carried him along toward his appointed rendezvous with death.

SURROUNDED BY HIS SOLDIERS in the shambles of the dining room, Seamus Kelly felt a sinking in his gut. His world was crumbling before his eyes, and the IRA commander knew that he would have to take control before the situation further deteriorated. His reputation was at stake and his life was riding on the line. And so far he had been unable to protect the men whom he was temporarily paid to serve.

The Chinese delegates were stretched out at his feet, a tablecloth stained with food and blood serving as their shroud. The dead weren't going anywhere, and Kelly had no feeling for them. His mind was on the shattered windows, plotting fields of fire, trajectories. He flinched at sight of movement in the dark outside, before he realized that sentries from his own detail were scouring the undergrowth in search of clues.

The bodies didn't bother Kelly. He had seen it all before—grown up with it, in fact. The images of violent death had followed him from childhood in Belfast until they had become the focus of his life. And it was not the bodies, but rather the beginnings of a certain *fear* inside, that made the IRA commander angry now.

He was afraid, all right. He could admit it to himself, but he could not afford to let it show. His men depended on him, and his life depended on the image he was able to project. He was a soldier first and always, pledged to carry on his endless war against the odds, without a sign of fear or favor toward the enemy. A show of weakness would destroy him now, and Seamus Kelly wasn't ready yet to see his whole life slip away.

"I want a thorough sweep from east to west across the grounds," he told his second in command. "We'll drive the bastard toward the road and pin him against the cliffs. From there, he has nowhere left to go but down."

"I'll see it done. An' what about the others, then?"

"Their problem," Kelly growled. "We'll try to keep 'em safe an' sound, but if they want to leave..."

He left the sentence hanging, waved his soldiers off and watched them go. There would be nothing he could do about it if the delegates should bolt; he might have penned them up inside Cashel House with difficulty, but that wasn't part of his assignment. His job was to keep them secure, and failing that, to see them safely off the grounds in the event of an emergency.

Like now.

This qualified as an emergency, all right, and he would not blame the delegates if they should leave en masse. The Chinese were already packing up their things, intent on getting out while they were able, and unless the IRA commander missed his guess, the other delegations would be close behind. The meeting was a bust, and anything Joe Scalish had accomplished at the start was crumbling now.

It was the first excuse for smiling that Seamus Kelly had discovered since he took the job at Cashel House. He hated Scalish and the rest for what they were, these parasites. It would not disturb him in the least if all of them went up in smoke, except that he had been employed to see that they were safe.

He worried more about the Russian than anything. His leading source of arms, of ready cash, was on the line, together with his reputation as a man who got things done. If he could not protect a group of flabby-assed businessmen inside an armed estate, the Russian might look elsewhere when it came to funding raids, supplying arms for new offensives on the northern front. It had been such a simple job, and yet . . .

At once, with crystal clarity, he knew precisely who the enemy must be. The only man among the delegates who wore a martial air about him, who possessed the skill and the ability to pull this off. The slick professional who had slaughtered six armed men that morning, after they had tried to take him by surprise.

The man called Michael Black.

It didn't matter why he might be shooting up the conference; that would be Scalish's concern, the reasoning behind it all, once things were sorted out. As far as Kelly was concerned, the motives were irrelevant.

What counted was the who—and, now, the where.

They had to find the tall American and bring him down before he had the chance to strike again. There was a sort of bond between them now, at least in Kelly's eyes, and it would link them inextricably until the tie was cut, in death.

The recognition of his enemy was one thing.

The eradication of that enemy was something else again.

The IRA commander knew his life was riding on the line as he prepared to join his men in the dark gardens, searching for a man whom he had never met till yesterday. A man who held his future in the balance now.

And it was getting personal for Seamus Kelly, as personal as life and death itself.

20

Chan Yuen Fai surveyed the room once more, his cold eyes taking hasty inventory, making certain that his party had left nothing behind. When he was satisfied, he closed the door behind him, trailing his surviving comrades toward the checkout desk.

The Triad delegates were clearing out. The conference had cost too much, and it was over now as far as Chan and his companions were concerned. He would arrange for transportation of the bodies later. There was a madman out there, waiting in the darkness, armed with God knows what, and Chan did not intend to risk another confrontation on unfamiliar ground.

Scalish, the New York mobster, would be disappointed, even angry, but the Triad chief would deal with that later. He owed the mafioso something for his wasted time and money, for his wounded friends, but he would have a lifetime to select the most appropriate revenge. Providing that he made it off the grounds of Cashel House alive, of course. Assuming they were not ambushed before they reached the car.

Chan slipped a hand inside his jacket, felt the automatic pistol's reassuring weight inside the waistband of his slacks. He was prepared to use it if they should be interfered with anywhere along their short walk to the car; both his companions were similarly armed. Scalish or his Soviet accomplice had better not try to stop them now.

Chan thought of his ancient enemies, the Vietnamese, and wondered if they might have been involved with the fiasco in the dining room. For many years, Hanoi had scrutinized his rich narcotics trade with hungry eyes, and if they could eliminate the major Triad leader here in a single sweep, they would be that much closer to the victory they craved. Chan wondered if the sniper had been Vietnamese.

The Japanese were hungry, too, and Chan had learned to fear the brash, impulsive soldiers of the Yakuza. They thrived on violence, turning on their own when there were no wars left to fight outside the family, assassinating rivals even when a peaceful settlement might be easier. The self-styled samurai were dangerous to everyone who came in contact with them, and the Triad chieftain was not ruling out anybody as suspects in the killing of his friends.

The tall American had tried to warn him, and Chan had listened with respect. But there had been assurances from Scalish, from the rest, and violence seemed remote amid the greenery of County Galway. Michael Black had hinted at the possibility of treachery afoot, but Chan had been complacent, putting all his faith in someone else's system of security.

It was a grim mistake that he would not repeat.

His party cleared the registration desk and was halfway to the door when Scalish called from the lounge.

"Hey, wait a second! What's the hurry?"

Chan did not slow down, but Scalish caught him at the threshold, tugging at his sleeve.

"Hold on," the mafioso whined. "You can't just leave like this."

"I can. I am."

"We've still got business here."

"No more."

"Now wait a minute, dammit!"

Scalish gripped his arm above the elbow and spun him. The new York mobster was about to speak when he felt the automatic's muzzle jammed against his rib cage, beneath his heart. A sidelong glance revealed two other weapons leveled at his face.

Scalish spread his empty hands and stepped back toward the lounge.

"Okay," he sneered. "Go on and throw it all away. If this is how you operate, you couldn't go the distance, anyhow."

Chan took a step in his direction, held the pistol close beneath the mafioso's chin.

"You have betrayed our trust," he told Joe Scalish, almost whispering. "The blood of our companions rests on you. It is a debt that we will someday find the method to repay."

No answer from New York, but he had paled and Chan could see his hands were trembling as he backed away from Scalish, homing on the exit.

A pair of floodlights lit the gravel drive in front of Cashel House, but Chan and his companions quickly left the glare behind, jogging as they reached the sloping track that led to the sunken parking lot. Another thirty yards and they would find a measure of security inside their rented car. Chan would not feel completely safe until they left the grounds. He kept the automatic pistol in his hand, a talisman against the darkness that surrounded them.

They were almost to their car before he realized they were not alone.

A man shape, then another and another, rose from a squat sedan parked beside their own. The men were mere silhouettes and Chan could not make out their features, but his eyes caught something in their stature, in their stance.

"You leave so soon?"

He recognized the accent instantly, and knew that the Yakuza had found him. No sign of any weapons yet, but they were shifting and spreading out, as if anticipating trouble from the Triad delegates.

Chan didn't plan to disappoint them.

"Our business here is done," he said, picking out the tallest of the shadows as his target, easing off the auto-loader's safety with his thumb.

"It is unfortunate about your friends."

Chan held his ground, following the movement of his target as it shifted to the left.

"I am surprised you break and run so easily."

Enough.

Chan brought up the automatic and squeezed off in rapid-fire. Beyond the blinding muzzle-flash, he saw the shadow figure topple. Then his friends were firing at the silhouetted targets.

The Yakuza were answering with weapons of their own, and Chan was suddenly aware of other enemies on his flank. He tracked a running target, was about to fire, but staggered under the impact of a bullet drilling through his shoulder, in and out, driving him against the fender of the rented Citroën. He felt the pistol slipping from his grasp and scrambled to retrieve it in the strobe-lit darkness of the parking lot.

He had retrieved it and was about to raise it when an automatic weapon ripped the night apart, eviscerating the darkness with a jagged muzzle-flash. The gunner stitched a line of death from left to right and back again, exploding flesh and window glass with fine impartiality, his stray rounds plunking into fenders, trunks, doors.

The last burst found a hot spot. Chan was watching as a squat VW reared up in an oily fireball, settling slowly back to earth. The flames, spreading to the shrubbery and to other cars, provided grim illumination of the battle-field.

Chan caught a fleeting glimpse of the man in black: a tall man, muscular, athletic, dressed in Ninja black and carrying an automatic rifle in his hands as if it was a toy.

One glimpse was all Chan needed to decide that there were other enemies out there beside the Yakuza.

The flames were spreading swiftly now, and Chan began to drag himself along the sloping gravel path, retreating toward the relative security of Cashel House. If his companions were alive, they would be fending for themselves, as Chan was forced to do. A leader's first responsibility was to survive.

And that, Chan realized, might be no easy task.

MACK BOLAN FED THE M-16 another magazine, moving to put ground between himself and the inferno of the parking lot. Three cars were burning now, the bullet-punctured Saab among them. But the matter of his transportation out could wait. For the moment, survival was the soldier's top priority.

He could hear the sentries closing on his last position, homing on the flames, the sounds of gunfire, and he froze among the shadows, taking full advantage of the undergrowth. The IRA commandos, intent on learning what had happened in the parking lot, were getting careless in their haste. They did not take the time required for a determined search, and one of them nearly touched Bolan as he passed by.

Another sputtering of shots; Bolan surmised that someone—Yakuza or Triad—had mistaken the security patrol for enemies. A short, staccato answer from the weapons of the sentries and the night was still again, except for the insistent, hungry crackling of the flames.

He made his move, a gliding shadow with the firelight at his back, retreating down the narrow track and immediately doubling back toward the hotel. He still had business there with Gladnikov, and the confusion of the shootout in the parking lot might give him all the edge required to get inside.

Provided that he did not run into an errant sentry.

Provided that his luck held firm.

But it was not a lucky night at Cashel House—for Bridget Chambers, for the Triad leader, Chan—or for the Executioner.

He heard the sentry coming, swung the automatic rifle onto target and squeezed off a burst. The tumblers cut a ragged pattern through the undergrowth, and there was thrashing in there now, a squeal of startled pain before the quick, reflexive fire came sizzling in.

He jumped into a shoulder roll and continued until he was beneath the overhanging shrubbery, the rifle searching for a target in the dark. He spotted three muzzle-flashes laying down a rough triangulated fire, and Bolan took them each in turn, with short, precision bursts from left to right.

The nearest gunner took his burst waist high, and lost it in a spinning dervish-dance, his weapon firing blindly toward the sky. The Executioner homed in on number two, a crouching figure to his left, who was firing from the hip. A spiral burst eviscerated him and punched him over backward, sprawling, his combat boots protruding out into the trail.

Number three was breaking for it. He burst from cover, laying down a screen of cover fire, retreating into darkness with reckless speed. A root reached out to trip him and the guy went down, assisted by a lethal burst from Bolan's M-16, the tumblers exploding in a line from crotch to throat.

Ignoring the established trail, Bolan plunged headlong through the undergrowth, with ferns and branches slashing at his face, his chest. No silent passage here, but he was running out of time. He would not allow the Soviet to get away.

The forest closed about him, swallowed him, and he was gone.

SCALISH FOUND ALEXEI GLADNIKOV sipping brandy in the bar, one eye on the barmaid, who had spent the past ten minutes polishing a single glass. She wasn't going anywhere and she seemed to recognize that, but she was bearing up, refusing to allow a show of weakness. Gladnikov respected her for that, and he was almost sorry that the girl would have to die.

As for Joe Scalish, that was something else again.

The capo from New York was muttering and cursing to himself before he reached the bar, and now he let himself explode, as if Alexei Gladnikov was one of his subordinates.

"What kinda fuckin' deal is this?" the mafioso asked, not waiting for an answer, not apparently desiring one. "The friggin' Chinese delegation's gone. The yellow bastards all pulled guns on me, for cryin' out loud. Can you figure that?"

Alexei shrugged and took another sip of brandy, savoring the rich liqueur.

"We got some kinda war down in the parking lot, I guess you know that, huh? An' all the other delegates are bailing out like there was no tomorrow."

"There may not be," Alexei told him calmly, setting down his snifter on the bar.

"How's that?"

"Tomorrow, Joseph. They might very well be right. There may be no tomorrow."

"What the hell—"

The Makarov 9 mm automatic pistol was an old and trusted friend. Alexei drew it from his waistband with a flourish, leveling it at the New York mafioso's chest.

"No man is guaranteed tomorrow, Joseph." He enjoyed the sudden fear reflected in the mobster's eyes. "You disappoint me greatly. So much money wasted. So much preparation."

"But it wasn't *me*! Goddammit, can't you get that through your head? It's not my fault!"

"Have courage, Joseph. Be a man."

"Goddammit!"

Scalish bolted, spinning on his heel and racing for the exit, against all odds. Alexei stroked the Makarov's hair trigger, watched the crimson flower blossom between the mobster's shoulder blades, the impact lifting him, propelling him along. Another round, for luck. The explosion of his skull was like a cherry bomb inside a rotten cantaloupe. The body slithered forward on its mutilated face and came to rest against the opposite wall.

A crash of glass behind him brought the Russian swiveling about, his pistol raised and ready, level with the barmaid's face. The glass she had been polishing had shattered at her feet, and she was hyperventilating, the rosy blush of panic rising in her cheeks.

Alexei reached her in a single stride and dragged her bodily across the bar. He pressed the smoky muzzle of the Makarov against her cheek, below one eye, and whispered to her with a lover's urgency.

"Be still, my little dove." He caught her fragrance, and it instantly excited him. "You must accompany me outside. We will be going for a little drive."

She trembled in his grip but made no effort to resist as he pushed her in front of him along the corridor toward his room. A stop to get his baggage, to alert Dmitri that they would be leaving now, ahead of schedule, and he would be off. The lady would provide him with a shield outside, and possibly with some diversion on the drive to Shannon.

Alexei decided he would let Dmitri take the wheel while he relaxed and found some welcome recreation with the new addition to his entourage. There would be ample time and opportunity to dump her body later, when he was finished with her.

This one had neither Bridget's poise nor cunning beauty, but she had the suppleness of youth and that would do. She was a consolation prize to make up for the grim fiasco that the County Galway meeting had become. Alexei needed something to lift his spirits, and this girl would fill his momentary needs.

He would not contemplate the rest of it—the aftermath report to Moscow—for a day or two. He needed breathing room, some time to think of a way to disguise his failure, camouflage his losses.

Alexei Gladnikov had lived through worse—the purges of Stalin, for example—but the times were changing faster than the faces on the Politburo, and it wouldn't hurt to have some insurance in his pocket, just in case, backup plans, perhaps, if he could think of one before he filed his next report. Something to make disaster carry the aroma of success. He was a master at his craft, and he would find a way to salvage something from the rubble.

But first he had to make it off the grounds alive, and from the sounds of gunfire in the garden, drawing closer by the moment, that might be the hardest task of all. The sentries were engaged in battle—with an enemy of substance, or their own imaginations—and it mattered little, either way. All targets looked alike at night.

Evacuating Cashel House would not be easy. The Russian was counting on the barmaid to be a bargaining tool if they were stopped along the way. She was expendable—as was Dmitri, if it came to that. Alexei Gladnikov was looking out for number one.

21

Seamus Kelly checked the action on his automatic rifle, finally satisfied, and turned toward the darkness of the trees. He didn't like these gardens, accustomed as he was to urban war, the killing ground of Ulster's streets and alleyways. He had a feeling for the pavement, for the darkness of a city, which is somehow never quite as dark as midnight in the tractless countryside. The IRA commander knew that he was only yards from the hotel, its lights ablaze, and yet he might as easily have been on the dark side of the moon.

It wasn't fear that gripped him now, he told himself, but simple unfamiliarity with the terrain. Before his mind had formed the thought, he recognized it for a lie, and the embarrassment of realizing that he was afraid made Kelly angry, dangerous.

A leader could afford his caution, certainly. Discretion was a must for any true guerrilla in the modern world. But fear was something else again, debilitating, murderous. It would destroy him if he let it grow inside, devouring his courage like a cancer of the soul.

It was the recognition of his fear, as well as his sense of duty, which had drawn him out, rifle in hand, to face the enemy. He might as easily have left his men to do the job, with none the wiser of his motives, but he couldn't hide forever from himself. *He* would have known, and that was all that mattered in the last analysis. He would have proved himself a coward to himself, and Seamus Kelly could not tolerate that.

From the cradle on, he had been raised on revolution, and from the time that he could heft a brick, a bottle bomb, he had been fighting in the ranks of Northern Ireland's partisans with single-minded zeal. He had participated in his first assassination at fifteen, as lookout, and had soloed for the first time four years later, by murdering a Tommy who had lingered in an Ulster alley to relieve himself. How many others had there been over the years? The twenty-seven that he counted privately, of course, and the hundreds of others who had fallen in the riots, snipings, car-bomb detonations.

Seamus Kelly had enough blood on his soul to float a battleship, and none of it had ever preyed upon his mind. He was a soldier with a cause, and it was too bad if the innocent occasionally got caught in his war. When Kelly met his maker, he would hold his head up high, defend his case—and pray that God was not an Englishman.

But here and now, the IRA commander was afraid.

He did not recognize his enemy beyond the face and bogus name. What drove this Michael Black to risk his life, to slaughter others here at Cashel House? The answer was simplicity itself, of course. The man was fighting for a cause.

The Irishman could understand that much, and it was all he had to know. It told him that his enemy would not withdraw until his job was done, that he would sacrifice himself if necessary to achieve his goal. And that, in turn, informed the IRA commander that he had a desperate battle on his hands.

How many dead so far? He didn't like to think about the numbers yet, and they were far from final, anyway. The two Chinese, another half a dozen in the parking lot, no less than four of his commandos up to now. All that in twenty minutes, and he knew with unrelenting certainty that Michael Black would soon be returning to the hotel.

Whatever drove him to his rampage rested there, and he would seek it out with grim determination.

So far, the solitary warrior showed a grim ability to hold his own against the odds.

It might have been the woman's death that set Black off, Kelly conjectured. The IRA commander had suspected Gladnikov of butchering the woman, his suspicion mounting to a certainty as he observed the Russian impassively studying her remains. She was the woman he had loved—at least, the woman who had shared his bed—and he had turned away from her eviscerated form without a backward glance. The Russian's eyes had locked with Kelly's for an instant, and the IRA commander saw that they were dead, as lifeless—*soulless*—as a stone.

So Michael Black was killing for revenge, and something else.

The rest of it was unimportant now, for Seamus Kelly understood revenge. He knew it made men reckless when they could least afford to let their feelings take the lead. A reckless man was easier to kill than one who kept his feelings under tight control, and Kelly saw a glimmer of hope in the darkness. If the American relied upon his feelings, they would have him soon, and it would all be over but the mopping up.

Something stirred in the undergrowth to Kelly's left, and he shifted to confront the new activity as Michael Black emerged from cover, dressed in black, his hands and face discolored, carrying the rifle lifted from the soldier he had killed inside. The target hesitated, glancing all around, braced to run, a frozen silhouette in Kelly's sights. Then both were shaken by a sudden crash in the brush, a rising shout and the explosion of erratic gunfire close at hand.

A squad of Kelly's troopers burst from cover on his right, their weapons blazing from the hip as they bore down on Michael Black. Kelly was already swinging back, his finger tightening around the trigger, ready for the kill, when he discovered that his prey had disappeared.

The man in black was gone.

Another heartbeat, and an automatic weapon answered those of his commandos, cutting through their loose formation from the side, a dozen yards from where the man in black had previously stood. Could he have moved that fast? That far?

The IRA commander bolted, homing on the faint suggestion of a muzzle-flash beneath the trees, ignoring his commandos and the fact that they were dying on the grass less than twenty feet away. He heard their screams and recognized their pain, abruptly silenced by another burst of gunfire from the undergrowth, but he was moving on, oblivious to everything except his quarry.

He had a chance if he was swift enough and sure enough to pull it off. Another moment now, and he would be within effective range. His target would be just beyond this hedge, perhaps reloading from the fusillade that had eliminated four of Kelly's best.

The stupid bastards. They had blundered in like amateurs and paid the price. Good riddance, then.

The IRA commander braced himself, tightly gripping the M-16, his muscles straining toward the jump. Go on! The only way to conquer fear is to confront it directly, and club it down.

He leaped, a thrashing, crashing figure in the undergrowth, as silent as a rhino in a china shop. He squeezed the trigger of his rifle blindly as he cleared the hedge, his tumblers scything down a stand of ferns and riddling tree trunks. Teeth clenched, he swept the rifle back and forth, from right to left and back again, excited by the sound and smell of it, the proximity of violent death. The grim excitement overrode his fear and made him whole.

Until he realized that he was firing into empty air.

The man in black was gone. Again.

A whisper in the sudden, ringing silence told the IRA commander he had been flanked. He didn't have to see the shadow gliding up behind him, didn't have to feel the muzzle of the automatic rifle pressed against his spine.

He was as good as dead.

And there was nothing left to do but play it out.

He twisted, dropping to a crouch and squeezing off, aware within the half a heartbeat left that something was terribly, irrevocably wrong.

His rifle wouldn't fire.

He had already emptied out the magazine, assassinating underbrush. Annihilating fear.

He recognized the man in black, and sensed that under other circumstances, in another time, they might have wound up fighting side by side. But this was all the time they would ever have, and it was over now.

"So do it then," the IRA commander said.

Those were his dying words.

CAUTIOUS BY NATURE, Alexei Gladnikov allowed Dmitri to precede him through the doors of the hotel. The little man was burdened down with bags, and he would make an easy target if a sniper should be waiting in the dark. He was expendable, of course, and always glad to serve.

Alexei followed, with the woman clutched in front of him, her closeness titillating now. He held the Makarov against her cheek, reminding her that he possessed the power of life and death, inspiring her to tremble in a way that always turned him on. It was an aphrodisiac for Gladnikov.

It had been good with Bridget before she cheated him in death. It could be better with the barmaid, tender as she was, unused to mortal terror—but he had to wait. Survival was the top priority right now, and while they lingered on the grounds at Cashel House, there was a chance that he would not survive.

A cautious agent never stayed behind to face the enemy when he could get away. It would not do to compromise his cover, his effectiveness, by lingering about the danger zone a moment longer than was absolutely necessary. He was clearing out, and as for the remaining delegates, well, as they said in the United States, it was every man for himself.

Sniffing the smoke from the car fires in the parking lot, Gladnikov was thankful he had hidden his own machine away from the others, ready for a swift escape. The BMW would accommodate the three of them and whisk them off to Shannon while the others battled for their lives and waited for the Garda to arrive. A nice predicament for all concerned—except the Soviets, of course.

No one could prove that he had been here, that he had anything to do with terrorism or the KGB or *anything*. He was invisible, unknown to CIA and MI-5, to FBI and Interpol, a faceless man who could traverse the world, infecting populations with the germs of revolution, crime, unrest. He was a master at the game.

They had killed the outside floodlights, bringing darkness down upon the lawn. Illumination from the dining room and several of the suites did little to disperse the shadows, but Alexei welcomed darkness now. It was a familiar friend and ally, suited to his purpose here. Ahead, Dmitri was a bobbing shadow, waddling beneath the burden of their luggage. The barmaid tensed, but did not try to escape as they moved toward the car.

Alexei recognized its sleek, familiar shape beneath the trees. Dmitri stripped back the cover, stowed it inside the trunk together with their bags, then returned with his key to open the door for Gladnikov and his companion. The little man was bent, his key in the lock, when suddenly he staggered and fell upon one knee.

The echo of the rifle shot was instantaneous and startling. Alexei whirled, holding the woman in front of him, as he heard a second shot and saw Dmitri's face disintegrate, the impact blowing him away.

The darkness mocked Alexei now. He felt hostile eyes upon him, staring through rifle sights, and there was almost nothing he could do. He thrust the Makarov against his captive's jaw with such ferocious pressure that she screamed.

"I have the woman," he informed the darkness. "I will kill her now, unless you show yourself."

"No deal."

The voice was low and quiet, grim. It was certainly American, and not completely unfamiliar, and yet in his present state Alexei could not place it with precision.

"You force my hand. I have no choice."

"You've always got a choice," the night replied.

Alexei figured he had a chance, if he could stall the sniper long enough. Slowly, he started moving toward the car.

"The woman's life is in your hands."

"*Your* life is in my hands," the enemy retorted, sounding closer now.

Alexei knew he had to move swiftly if his plan was to succeed. Another instant to brace himself, and he propelled the woman forward with a straight-arm shove toward the faceless voice. He raised the Makarov and snapped a ringing double-punch across her shoulder, toward the darkened trees, already lunging for the BMW's door—and found it locked.

Dmitri's key was dangling in the lock, where dying fingers had released it moments earlier. Alexei grabbed it, twisted it, felt the latching mechanism disengage. Then a burst of automatic fire exploded through the windshield, bullets whining off the BMW's bodywork, a single stunning round impacting on Alexei's shoulder, spinning him around and flinging him to the ground.

He huddled against the car, prayed it would shield him from the sniper's deadly fire. His wounded arm was numb, but he could feel the warmth and wetness of his blood inside his shirt. He had to move quickly or the enemy would find him and kill him.

Commanding almost superhuman strength, Alexei began a run toward the trees. Another burst erupted from the shadows as he cleared the car, but sheer momentum carried him beyond the line of fire, and he was gone, a reeling silhouette enveloped by the trees and undergrowth.

The Russian had no firm idea of where he was, still less of where he meant to go. It crossed his mind that he could reach the highway, flag a ride or something.

No time to think of the specifics now. If he slowed down, if he allowed the enemy to overtake him, he was dead.

Survival was the only thing that mattered now.

Survival, so that he could fight another day.

But as he ran, Alexei knew he might not see another day. Tonight might be the only time he had.

The understanding brought him fear, and with it came the pain.

CROUCHING BESIDE THE GIRL, Mack Bolan found that she was still alive, unharmed. He left her there, as safe as anywhere in Cashel House this night, and followed the retreating figure of Alexei Gladnikov between the dark trees.

The Russian had surprised him with his energy, his strength. An average man would not have found the fortitude to make a break with half his shoulder blown away. But this one was no ordinary man. He had already proved as much with Bridget.

He was no man at all.

A savage, and driven now by primal fear, a need to escape. His wound was serious, but he could still survive, with luck, some help, and Bolan meant to help the lethal odds along. The KGB agent would not be leaving Cashel House alive unless he managed to outgun the Executioner.

So far, the luck had been with Bolan, and he was thankful that he had encountered Gladnikov before he slipped inside his car, his aide behind the wheel. It would have been a sticky situation with the woman there, inside—but it had never come about.

Inside the garden now, surrounded by the night, Mack Bolan heard his quarry crashing through the underbrush ahead. The jungle was familiar ground, in Ireland or in Vietnam, and he could feel its rhythms reaching for him, calling him to join the dance. No time for stealth, when life was running out through ragged wounds with every passing second now. The Russian had his bearings, knew the general direction of the highway, but getting there was something else again.

Hanging back, the soldier followed, allowing Gladnikov to make the noise for both of them. The IRA commandos still might be prowling, anxious for a shot at any errant sound. If they encountered Gladnikov, they would waste him on the spot. If not, well, Bolan didn't plan on letting anybody nurse the Russian back to health.

Cautiously he followed Gladnikov along the narrow path, every combat sense alert to any sign of danger in the darkness. From all appearances, the sentries were distracted by the gunplay at the hotel building, closing in to seal it off, preventing any of the other delegates from getting out. That suited Bolan fine; he needed room to run, and the distraction meant that he would have some time alone with Gladnikov.

Intent on closing with his adversary, the hunter gradually increased his pace. The smell of blood was in his nostrils, and he needed contact with the enemy to purge the anger that had built inside him since discovering Bridget's corpse.

The Executioner did not conduct his war for personal revenge, although its roots were based in family tragedy. Before the first campaign was over, he had learned the universal nature of the enemy, the savage threat it posed to all mankind. With that knowledge came a cool determination to conduct his war professionally, outside the heat of passion that could breed mistakes.

But he was basking in that heat right now, drawing energy from Bridget's senseless death. It drove him on along the narrow track, following the death sounds of his wounded prey.

Gladnikov was closing on the highway, but he was veering north, following a path that climbed inexorably toward the garden's highest point. He might have lost direction, or he might have changed his mind, selected somewhere else to make his final stand. In any case, he was proceeding toward the hilltop overlooking Cashel Bay.

The soldier followed, grim, implacable.

He was accustomed to the hunt, and here, amid the man-made forest, he was feeling right at home.

A sudden stillness in the trees ahead told him that his prey had gone to ground. He slowed; veering off the track, he moved silently among the trees until he reached the summit of the hill. Above him, pale as ivory, the moon looked down on County Galway and the hunt.

He found Alexei waiting for him on a wooden bench. Winded by his run, the Russian was breathing heavily, his head slumped forward, chin supported on his chest. The moonlight glistened on his jacket, saturated with a vast amount of blood, and Bolan knew he was as good as dead already.

And still, it was not good enough.

The soldier showed himself, intent upon the Makarov that lay beside Gladnikov on the rough-hewn bench as he approached to stand before his prey. The Russian rolled his head back, forced his eyes to focus on the apparition dressed in black.

"At last."

"At last," the Executioner agreed.

"The woman?"

"Yes."

Gladnikov nodded weakly, forced a smile. "Of course. Americans are so Victorian."

"She did you in," Bolan told him, speaking slowly, letting it sink in.

The Russian frowned, apparently exhausted by the effort.

"She was Interpol," the soldier told him, gauging the reaction, realizing that Gladnikov hadn't known. Not even now. "She had you covered, guy."

The lips were moving, but the man from Russia couldn't seem to find his voice. It didn't matter, anyway. He knew, and that was all that counted for the Executioner.

He raised the M-16 and put a single round between those fading eyes at point-blank range. The balding head snapped back, its scalp vaporized, and Gladnikov relaxed in death, a sluggish lateral collapse that left him draped across the bench.

The soldier left him there, and looked up at the heavens, the moon. It shone on all of them—on Gladnikov, on Bridget Chambers, on the Executioner.

Would it be shining, too, at home?

He turned away from Gladnikov and started back. It was a long walk down.

EPILOGUE

The Aerlingus trans-Atlantic flight surprised him with a Tarzan film. It was a modern remake with a twist; the jungle king comes home to England and the family he never knew he had. No happy ending there, however; once ensconced in Greystoke Manor, he discovers that he cannot adjust to civilized society. In the closing reel he returns to his savage jungle home, to seek a solitary life among the predators.

Mack Bolan sympathized, because he had been there. Except that he had started out in civilized society and voluntarily sought the jungle in his youth, a warrior pledged to tame the predators and purge the savages. He had come home to tragedy, and learned a bitter truth about the jungle.

It was everywhere. In Vietnam. In the United States. In County Galway.

And for the Executioner, there could be no escape.

He removed the plastic earphones and stowed them in the pocket of the seat in front of him. As the closing credits rolled, he closed his eyes and sought the momentary respite of sleep.

But there was no escape, and Bolan knew that well enough. His dreams were bloody treks across the killing ground, no end in sight. Reality was an extension of those dreams, as dreaming had become a grim extension of reality.

The Executioner was going home, but he was not escaping from the jungle. It was waiting for him, stateside, anxious to receive him, face him off against the latest crop of predators.

He slept, and in his sleep, he smiled.

The jungle king would not have had it any other way.

MORE ACTION!
MORE SUSPENSE!
NEW LOOK!

THE EXECUTIONER

MACK BOLAN

Beginning in July, watch out for America's number-one hero, Mack Bolan, in more spectacular, more gut-wrenching missions.

The Executioner continues to live large in bigger, bolder stories that can only be told in 256 pages.

Get into the heart of the man and the heart of the action with the first big entry, **The Trial**.

In this gripping adventure, Bolan is captured and placed on trial for his life—accused by the government he had sworn to serve. And the prosecution is hunting for the soldier's head.

Gold Eagle Books is giving readers what they asked for. You've never read action-adventure like this before!

ME

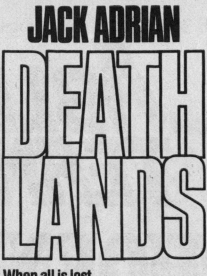

MORE ADVENTURE NEXT MONTH WITH

MACK BOLAN

#90 Blood Heat Zero

Frozen Hell

Mack Bolan, exhausted by the firestorm that is his life, decides to take a well-deserved R and R. But instead of some tropical resort, the Executioner plans to challenge nature's whims in the depths of an Icelandic glacier.

On a perilous trip beneath the polar ice cap, he makes a discovery so startling, it is tantamount to an act of war.

And the innocent vacation becomes a hunt—with Bolan as the prey.

---

4 FREE BOOKS
1 FREE GIFT

NO RISK
NO OBLIGATION
NO KIDDING

SPECIAL LIMITED-TIME OFFER

Mail to **Gold Eagle Reader Service**

In the U.S.
901 Fuhrmann Blvd.
P.O. Box 1394
Buffalo, N.Y. 14240-1394

In Canada
P.O. Box 2800, Station A
5170 Yonge St.,
Willowdale, Ont. M2N 6J3

YEAH! Rush me 4 free Gold Eagle novels and my free mystery bonus. Then send me 6 brand-new novels every other month as they come off the presses. Bill me at the low price of $2.25 each—a 10% saving off the retail price. There are no shipping, handling or other hidden costs. There is no minimum number of books I must buy. I can always return a shipment and cancel at any time. Even if I never buy another book from Gold Eagle, the 4 free novels and the mystery bonus are mine to keep forever.

166-BPM-BP6S

Name   (PLEASE PRINT)

Address   Apt. No.

City   State/Prov.   Zip/Postal Code

Signature (If under 18, parent or guardian must sign)

This offer is limited to one order per household and not valid to present subscribers. Price is subject to change.

166-BPM-BPGE   NO-SUB-1-RR